Praise for A. S. Byatt's

Little Black Book of Stories

"A storyteller who could keep a sultan on the edge of his throne for a thousand and one nights."
— *The New York Times Book Review*

"Scrumptious. . . . These are raw, tough, disruptive stories about memory, duty, madness, guilt, cruelty and loss, stories that grope and reel, that throb with secret longings, secret histories, artistic yearnings and the thrashes and groans of a stinking damnation in the underbrush." — *The Miami Herald*

"Her finest collection yet. . . . Bleak then surprisingly funny, very dark indeed then full of inconceivable sources of light." — *The Guardian* (London)

"Beautifully crafted. . . . [*Little Black Book of Stories*] prods at the tender points where art, pain, and desire intersect." — *Financial Times*

"A potent alchemy of magic, horror and sensual delight." — *Elle*

"Captivating . . . disturbing yet funny . . . an utterly compelling read."   —*Harper's Bazaar*

"A delightful surprise. . . . A heady infusion of mythology and everyday life, with a strong undercurrent of horror. . . . Moving, thought-provoking, witty, and shocking all at once."
                              —*The Sunday Telegraph* (London)

"Haunting . . . astonishing . . . vivid . . . moving. . . . [Byatt] is an athlete of the imagination, breaking barriers without apparent effort."   —*The Nation*

"A sophisticated and powerfully realized work. . . . A bravura performance of imaginative artistry."
                      —*The Times Literary Supplement* (London)

A. S. BYATT

Little Black Book of Stories

A. S. Byatt is the author of numerous novels, including *A Whistling Woman* and *Possession,* which was awarded the Booker Prize in 1990. She has also written two novellas, published together as *Angels & Insects,* four previous collections of shorter works, and several works of nonfiction. Educated at Cambridge, she was a senior lecturer in English at University College, London. She lives in London.

INTERNATIONAL

Little Black
Book of Stories

Little Black Book of Stories

❦

A. S. BYATT

Vintage International
Vintage Books
A Division of Random House, Inc.
New York

The Library of Congress has cataloged the Knopf edition as follows:
Byatt, A.S. (Antonia Susan), [date]
Little black book of stories / A. S. Byatt.—1st ed.
p. cm.
Contents: The thing in the forest—Body art—A stone woman—
Raw material—The pink ribbon.
I. Title.
PR6052.Y2L58 2004
823'.914—dc22
2003065940

Vintage ISBN: 978-1-4000-7560-7

Author photograph © Michael Trevillion
Book design by Virginia Tan

www.vintagebooks.com

146122990

*For Anna Nadotti and Fausto Galuzzi,
and for Melanie Walz.*

Contents

The Thing
in the Forest

THERE WERE ONCE two little girls who saw, or believed they saw, a thing in a forest. The two little girls were evacuees, who had been sent away from the city by train, with a large number of other children. They all had their names attached to their coats with safety-pins, and they carried little bags or satchels, and the regulation gas-mask. They wore knitted scarves and bonnets or caps, and many had knitted gloves attached to long tapes which ran along their sleeves, inside their coats, and over their shoulders and out, so that they could leave their ten woollen fingers dangling, like a spare pair of hands, like a scarecrow. They all had bare legs and scuffed shoes and wrinkled socks. Most had wounds on their knees in varying stages of freshness and scabbiness. They were at the age when children fall often and their knees were unprotected. With their suitcases, some of which were almost too big to carry, and their other impedimenta, a doll, a toy car, a comic, they were like a disorderly dwarf regiment, stomping along the platform.

The two little girls had not met before, and made friends on the train. They shared a square of chocolate, and took alternate bites at an apple. One gave the other the inside page of her *Beano*. Their names were Penny and Primrose. Penny was thin and dark and taller, possibly older, than Primrose, who was plump and blonde and curly. Primrose had bitten nails, and a velvet collar to her dressy green coat. Penny had a bloodless transparent paleness, a touch of blue in her fine lips. Neither of them knew where they were going, nor how long the journey might take. They did not even know why they were going, since neither of their mothers had quite known how to explain the danger to them. How do you say to your child, I am sending you away, because enemy bombs may fall out of the sky, because the streets of the city may burn like forest fires of brick and timber, but I myself am staying here, in what I believe may be daily danger of burning, burying alive, gas, and ultimately perhaps a grey army rolling in on tanks over the suburbs, or sailing its submarines up our river, all guns blazing? So the mothers (who did not resemble each other at all) behaved alike, and explained nothing, it was easier. Their daughters they knew were little girls, who would not be able to understand or imagine.

The girls discussed on the train whether it was a sort of holiday or a sort of punishment, or a bit of both. Penny had read a book about Boy Scouts, but the children on the train did not appear to be Brownies or Wolf Cubs, only a mongrel battalion of the lost. Both little girls had the idea that these were all perhaps *not very good* children, possibly being sent away for that reason. They were pleased to be able to define each other as "nice." They would stick together, they agreed. Try to sit together, and things.

THE TRAIN CRAWLED sluggishly further and further away from the city and their homes. It was not a clean train—the upholstery of their carriage had the dank smell of unwashed trousers, and the gusts of hot steam rolling backwards past their windows were full of specks of flimsy ash, and sharp grit, and occasional fiery sparks that pricked face and fingers like hot needles if you opened the window. It was very noisy too, whenever it picked up a little speed. The engine gave great bellowing sighs, and the invisible wheels underneath clicked rhythmically and monotonously, tap-tap-tap-CRASH, tap-tap-tap-CRASH. The window-panes were both grimy and misted up. The train stopped frequently, and when it stopped, they used their gloves to wipe rounds, through which they peered out at flooded fields, furrowed hillsides and tiny stations whose names were carefully blacked out, whose platforms were empty of life.

The children did not know that the namelessness was meant to baffle or delude an invading army. They felt—they did not think it out, but somewhere inside them the idea sprouted—that the erasure was because of them, because they were not meant to know where they were going or, like Hansel and Gretel, to find the way back. They did not speak to each other of this anxiety, but began the kind of conversation children have about things they really disliked, things that upset, or disgusted, or frightened them. Semolina pudding with its grainy texture, mushy peas, fat on roast meat. Listening to the stairs and the window-sashes creaking in the dark or the wind. Having your head held roughly back over the basin to have your hair washed, with cold water running down inside your liberty bodice. Gangs in playgrounds. They felt the pressure of all the other alien children in all the other carriages as a potential gang. They shared another square of chocolate, and licked their fingers, and looked out at a great white goose flapping its wings beside an inky pond.

The sky grew dark grey and in the end the train halted. The children got out, and lined up in a crocodile, and were led to a mud-coloured bus. Penny and Primrose managed to get a seat together, although it was over the wheel, and both of them began to feel sick as the bus bumped along snaking country lanes, under whipping branches, dark leaves on dark wooden arms on a dark sky, with torn strips of thin cloud streaming across a full moon, visible occasionally between them.

The Thing in the Forest

THEY WERE BILLETED temporarily in a mansion commandeered from its owner, which was to be arranged to hold a hospital for the long-term disabled, and a secret store of artworks and other valuables. The children were told they were there temporarily, until families were found to take them all into their homes. Penny and Primrose held hands, and said to each other that it would be wizard if they could go to the same family, because at least they would have each other. They didn't say anything to the rather tired-looking ladies who were ordering them about, because with the cunning of little children, they knew that requests were most often counter-productive, adults liked saying no. They imagined possible families into which they might be thrust. They did not discuss what they imagined, as these pictures, like the black station signs, were too frightening, and words might make some horror solid, in some magical way. Penny, who was a reading child, imagined Victorian dark pillars of severity, like Jane Eyre's Mr. Brocklehurst, or David Copperfield's Mr. Murdstone. Primrose imagined— she didn't know why—a fat woman with a white cap and round red arms who smiled nicely but made the children wear sacking aprons and scrub the steps and the stove. "It's like we were orphans," she said to Penny. "But we're not," Penny said. "If we manage to stick together . . ."

THE GREAT HOUSE had a double flight of imposing stairs to its front door, and carved griffins and unicorns on its balustrade. There was no lighting, because of the black-out. All the windows were shuttered. No welcoming brightness leaked across door or window-sill. The children trudged up the staircase in their crocodile, hung their coats on numbered makeshift hooks, and were given supper (Irish stew and rice pudding with a dollop of blood-red jam) before going to bed in long makeshift dormitories, where once servants had slept. They had camp-beds (military issue) and grey shoddy blankets. Penny and Primrose got beds together but couldn't get a corner. They queued to brush their teeth in a tiny washroom, and both suffered (again without speaking) suffocating anxiety about what would happen if they wanted to pee in the middle of the night, because the lavatory was one floor down, the lights were all extinguished, and they were a long way from the door. They also suffered from a fear that in the dark the other children would start laughing and rushing and teasing, and turn themselves into a gang. But that did not happen. Everyone was tired and anxious and orphaned. An uneasy silence, a drift of perturbed sleep, came over them all. The only sounds—from all parts of the great dormitory it seemed—were suppressed snuffles and sobs, from faces pressed into thin pillows.

The Thing in the Forest

When daylight came, things seemed, as they mostly do, brighter and better. The children were given breakfast in a large vaulted room. They sat at trestle tables, eating porridge made with water and a dab of the red jam, heavy cups of strong tea. Then they were told they could go out and play until lunch-time. Children in those days—wherever they came from— were not closely watched, were allowed to come and go freely, and those evacuated children were not herded into any kind of holding-pen, or transit camp. They were told they should be back for lunch at 12:30, by which time those in charge hoped to have sorted out their provisional future lives. It was not known how they would know when it was 12:30, but it was expected that—despite the fact that few of them had wrist-watches—they would know how to keep an eye on the time. It was what they were used to.

Penny and Primrose went out together, in their respectable coats and laced shoes, on to the terrace. The terrace appeared to them to be vast, and was indeed extensive. It was covered with a fine layer of damp gravel, stained here and there bright green, or invaded by mosses. Beyond it was a stone balustrade, with a staircase leading down to a lawn, which that morning had a quicksilver sheen on the lengthening grass. It was flanked by long flower-beds, full of over-blown annuals and damp clumps of stalks. A gardener would have noticed the beginnings of neglect, but these were urban little girls, and they noticed the jungly mass of wet stems, and the wet, vegetable smell. Across the lawn, which seemed considerably vaster than the vast terrace, was a sculpted yew hedge, with many twigs and shoots out of place and ruffled. In the middle of the hedge was a wicket-gate, and beyond the gate were trees, woodland, a forest, the little girls said to themselves.

"Let's go into the forest," said Penny, as though the sentence was required of her.

Primrose hesitated. Most of the other children were running up and down the terrace, scuffing their shoes in the gravel. Some boys were kicking a ball on the grass. The sun came right out, full from behind a hazy cloud, and the trees suddenly looked both gleaming and secret.

"OK," said Primrose. "We needn't go far."

"No. I've never been in a forest."

"Nor me."

"We ought to look at it, while we've got the opportunity," said Penny.

There was a very small child—one of the smallest—whose name, she told everyone, was Alys. With a *y,* she told those who could spell, and those who couldn't, which surely included herself. She was barely out of nappies. She was quite extraordinarily pretty, pink and white, with large pale blue eyes, and sparse little golden curls all over her head and neck, through which her pink skin could be seen. Nobody seemed to be in charge of her, no elder brother or sister. She had not quite managed to wash the tearstains from her dimpled cheeks.

She had made several attempts to attach herself to Penny and Primrose. They did not want her. They were excited about meeting and liking each other. She said now:

"I'm coming too, into the forest."

"No, you aren't," said Primrose.

"You're too little, you must stay here," said Penny.

"You'll get lost," said Primrose.

"You won't get lost. I'll come with you," said the little creature, with an engaging smile, made for loving parents and grandparents.

"We don't want you, you see," said Primrose.

"It's for your own good," said Penny.

Alys went on smiling hopefully, the smile becoming more of a mask.

"It will be all right," said Alys.

"Run," said Primrose.

They ran; they ran down the steps and across the lawn, and through the gate, into the forest. They didn't look back. They were long-legged little girls, not toddlers. The trees were silent round them, holding out their branches to the sun, breathing noiselessly.

PRIMROSE TOUCHED the warm skin of the nearest saplings, taking off her gloves to feel their cracks and knots. She exclaimed over the flaking whiteness and dusty brown of the silver birches, the white leaves of the aspens. Penny looked into the thick of the forest. There was undergrowth—a mat of brambles and bracken. There were no obvious paths. Dark and light came and went, inviting and mysterious, as the wind pushed clouds across the face of the sun.

"We have to be careful not to get lost," she said. "In stories, people make marks on tree-trunks, or unroll a thread, or leave a trail of white pebbles—to find their way back."

"We needn't go out of sight of the gate," said Primrose. "We could just explore a little bit."

They set off, very slowly. They went on tiptoe, making their own narrow passages through the undergrowth, which sometimes came as high as their thin shoulders. They were urban, and unaccustomed to silence. At first the absence of human noise filled them with a kind of awe, as though, while they would not have put it to themselves in this way, they had got to some original place, from which they, or those before them, had come, and which they therefore recognised. Then they began to hear the small sounds that were there. The chatter and repeated lilt and alarm of invisible birds, high up, further in. The hum and buzz of insects. Rustling in dry leaves, rushes of movement in thickets. Slitherings, dry coughs, sharp cracks. They went on, pointing out to each other creepers draped with glistening berries, crimson, black and emerald, little crops of toadstools, some scarlet, some ghostly-pale, some a dead-flesh purple, some like tiny parasols—and some like pieces of meat protruding from tree-trunks. They met blackberries, but didn't pick them, in case in this place they were dangerous or deceptive. They admired from a safe distance the stiff upright fruiting rods of the Lords and Ladies, packed with fat red berries. They stopped to watch spiders spin, swinging from twig to twig, hauling in their silky cables, reinforcing knots and joinings. They sniffed the air, which was full of a warm mushroom smell, and a damp moss smell, and a sap smell, and a distant hint of dead ashes.

DID THEY HEAR IT first or smell it first? Both sound and scent were at first infinitesimal and dispersed. Both gave the strange impression of moving in—in waves—from the whole perimeter of the forest. Both increased very slowly in volume, and both were mixed, a sound and a smell fabricated of many disparate sounds and smells. A crunching, a crackling, a crushing, a heavy thumping, combined with threshing and thrashing, and added to that a gulping, heaving, boiling, bursting steaming sound, full of bubbles and farts, piffs and explosions, swallowings and wallowings. The smell was worse, and more aggressive, than the sound. It was a liquid smell of putrefaction, the smell of maggoty things at the bottom of untended dustbins, the smell of blocked drains, and unwashed trousers, mixed with the smell of bad eggs, and of rotten carpets and ancient polluted bedding. The new, ordinary forest smells and sounds, of leaves and humus, fur and feathers, so to speak, went out like lights as the atmosphere of the thing preceded it. The two little girls looked at each other, and took each other's hand. Speechlessly and instinctively they crouched down behind a fallen tree-trunk, and trembled, as the thing came into view.

Its head appeared to form, or become first visible in the distance, between the trees. Its face—which was triangular—appeared like a rubbery or fleshy mask over a shapeless sprouting bulb of a head, like a monstrous turnip. Its colour was the colour of flayed flesh, pitted with wormholes, and its expression was neither wrath nor greed, but pure misery. Its most defined feature was a vast mouth, pulled down and down at the corners, tight with a kind of pain. Its lips were thin, and raised, like welts from whipstrokes. It had blind, opaque white eyes, fringed with fleshy lashes and brows like the feelers of sea-anemones. Its face was close to the ground, and moved towards the children between its forearms which were squat, thick, powerful and akimbo, like a cross between a monstrous washerwoman and a primeval dragon. The flesh on these forearms was glistening and mottled, every colour, from the green of mould to the red-brown of raw liver, to the dirty white of dry rot.

The rest of its very large body appeared to be glued

together, like still-wet papier-mâché, or the carapace of stones and straws and twigs worn by caddis-flies underwater. It had a tubular shape, as a turd has a tubular shape, a provisional amalgam. It was made of rank meat, and decaying vegetation, but it also trailed veils and prostheses of man-made materials, bits of wire-netting, foul dishcloths, wire-wool full of pan-scrubbings, rusty nuts and bolts. It had feeble stubs and stumps of very slender legs, growing out of it at all angles, wavering and rippling like the suckered feet of a caterpillar or the squirming fringe of a centipede. On and on it came, bending and crushing whatever lay in its path, including bushes, though not substantial trees, which it wound between, awkwardly. The little girls observed, with horrified fascination, that when it met a sharp stone, or a narrow tree-trunk, it allowed itself to be sliced through, flowed sluggishly round in two or three smaller worms, convulsed and reunited. Its progress was achingly slow, very smelly, and apparently very painful, for it moaned and whined amongst its other burblings and belchings. They thought it could not see, or certainly could not see clearly. It and its stench passed within a few feet of their tree-trunk, humping along, leaving behind it a trail of bloody slime and dead foliage, sucked to dry skeletons.

Its end was flat and blunt, almost transparent, like some earthworms.

When it had gone, Penny and Primrose, kneeling

on the moss and dead leaves, put their arms about each other, and hugged each other, shaking with dry sobs. Then they stood up, still silent, and stared together, hand in hand, at the trail of obliteration and destruction, which wound out of the forest and into it again. They went back, hand in hand, without looking behind them, afraid that the wicket-gate, the lawn, the stone steps, the balustrade, the terrace and the great house would be transmogrified, or simply not there. But the boys were still playing football on the lawn, a group of girls were skipping and singing shrilly on the gravel. They let go each other's hand, and went back in.

THEY DID NOT SPEAK to each other again.

THE NEXT DAY they were separated and placed with strange families. Their time in these families— Primrose was in a dairy farm, Penny was in a parsonage—did not in fact last very long, though then the time seemed slow-motion and endless. These alien families seemed like dream worlds into which they had strayed, not knowing the physical or social rules which constructed those worlds. Afterwards, if they remembered the evacuation it was as dreams are remembered, with mnemonics designed to claw back what fleets on waking. So Primrose remembered the sound of milk spurting in the pail, and Penny remembered the empty corsets of the vicar's wife, hanging bony on the line. They remembered dandelion clocks, but you can remember those from anywhere, any time. They remembered the thing they had seen in the forest, on the contrary, in the way you remember those very few dreams—almost all nightmares—which have the quality of life itself, not of fantasm, or shifting provisional scene-set. (Though what are dreams if not life itself?) They remembered too solid flesh, too precise a stink, a rattle and a soughing which thrilled the nerves and the cartilage of their growing ears. In the memory, as in such a dream, they felt, I cannot get out, this is a real thing in a real place.

THEY RETURNED from evacuation, like many evacuees, so early that they then lived through wartime in the city, bombardment, blitz, unearthly light and roaring, changed landscapes, holes in their world where the newly dead had been. Both lost their fathers. Primrose's father was in the Army, and was killed, very late in the war, on a crowded troop-carrier sunk in the Far East. Penny's father, a much older man, was in the Auxiliary Fire Service, and died in a sheet of flame in the East India Docks on the Thames, pumping evaporating water from a puny coil of hose. They found it hard, after the war, to remember these different men. The claspers of memory could not grip the drowned and the burned. Primrose saw an inane grin under a khaki cap, because her mother had a snapshot. Penny thought she remembered her father, already grey-headed, brushing ash off his boots and trouser-cuffs as he put on his tin hat to go out. She thought she remembered a quaver of fear in his tired face, and the muscles composing themselves into resolution. It was not much, what either of them remembered.

AFTER THE WAR, their fates were still similar and dissimilar. Penny's widowed mother embraced grief, closed her face and her curtains, moved stiffly, like an automat, and read poetry. Primrose's mother married one of the many admirers, visitors, dancing partners she had had before the ship went down, gave birth to another five children, and developed varicose veins and a smoker's cough. She dyed her blonde hair with peroxide when it faded. Both Primrose and Penny were only children who now, because of the war, lived in amputated or unreal families. Penny developed crushes on poetical teachers and in due course—she was clever—went to university, where she chose to study developmental psychology. Primrose had little education. She was always being kept off school to look after the others. She too dyed her blonde curls with peroxide when they turned mousy and faded. She got fat as Penny got thin. Neither of them married. Penny became a child psychologist, working with the abused, the displaced, the disturbed. Primrose did this and that. She was a barmaid. She worked in a shop. She went to help at various church crèches and Salvation Army reunions, and discovered she had a talent for story-telling. She became Aunty Primrose, with her own repertoire. She was employed to tell tales to kindergartens and entertain at children's parties. She was much in demand at Hallowe'en, and had her own circle of bright yellow plastic chairs in a local shopping mall, where she kept an eye on the children of burdened women, keeping them safe, offering them just a *frisson* of fear and terror that made them wriggle with pleasure.

THE HOUSE AGED differently. During this period of time—whilst the little girls became women—it was handed over to the Nation, which turned it into a living museum, still inhabited by the flesh and blood descendants of those who had built it, demolished it, flung out a wing, closed off a corridor. Guided tours took place in it, at regulated times. During these tours, the ballroom and intimate drawing-rooms were fenced off with crimson twisted ropes on little brass one-eyed pedestals. The bored and the curious peered in at four-poster beds and pink silk *fauteuils*, at silver-framed photographs of wartime Royalty, and crackling crazing Renaissance and Enlightenment portraits of long-dead queens and solemn or sweetly musing ancestors. In the room where the evacuees had eaten their rationed meals, the history of the house was displayed, on posters, in glass cases, with helpful notices, and opened copies of old diaries and records. There were reproductions of the famous paintings which had lain here in hiding during the war. There was a plaque to the dead of the house: a gardener, an under-gardener, a chauffeur and a second son. There were photographs of military hospital beds, and of nurses pushing wheelchairs in the grounds. There was no mention of the evacuees whose presence appeared to have been too brief to have left any trace.

THE TWO WOMEN met in this room on an autumn day in 1984. They had come with a group, walking in a chattering crocodile behind a guide, and had lingered amongst the imagery and records, rather than going on to eavesdrop on the absent ladies and gentlemen whose tidy clutter lay on coffee tables and escritoires. They prowled around the room, each alone with herself, in opposite directions, without acknowledging each other's presence. Both their mothers had died that spring, within a week of each other, though this coincidence was unknown to them. It had made both of them think of taking a holiday, and both had chosen that part of the world. Penny was wearing a charcoal trouser suit and a black velvet hat. Primrose wore a floral knit long jacket over a shell-pink cashmere sweater, over a rustling long skirt with an elastic waist, in a mustard-coloured tapestry print. Her hips and bosom were bulky. They coincided because both of them, at the same moment, half saw an image in a medieval-looking illustrated book. Primrose thought it was a very old book. Penny assumed it was nineteenth-century mock-medieval. It showed a knight, on foot, in a forest, lifting his sword to slay something. The knight shone on the rounded slope of the page, in the light, which caught the gilding on his helmet and sword-belt. It was not possible to see what was being slain. This was because, both in the tangled vegetation of the image, and in the way the book was displayed in the case, the enemy, or victim, was in shadows.

Neither of them could read the ancient (or pseudo-ancient) black letter of the text beside the illustration. There was a typed explanation, or description, under the book, done with a faded ribbon and uneven pressure of the keys. They had to lean forward to read it, and to see what was worming its way into, or out of, the deep spine of the book, and that was how they came to see each other's face, close up, in the glass which was both transparent and reflective. Their transparent reflected faces lost detail—cracked lipstick, pouches, fine lines of wrinkles—and looked both younger and greyer, less substantial. And that is how they came to recognise each other, as they might not have done, plump face to bony face. They breathed each other's names, Penny, Primrose, and their breath misted the glass, obscuring the knight and his opponent. I could have died, I could have wet my knickers, said Penny and Primrose afterwards to each other, and both experienced this still moment as pure, dangerous shock. But they stayed there, bent heads together, legs trembling, knees knocking, and read the caption, which was about the Loathly Worm, which, tradition held, had infested the countryside and had been killed more than once by scions of that house, Sir Lionel, Sir Boris, Sir Guillem. The Worm, the typewriter had tapped out, was an English Worm, not a European dragon, and like most such worms, was wingless. In some sightings it was reported as having vestigial legs, hands or feet. In others it was limbless. It had, in monstrous form, the capacity of common or garden worms to sprout new heads or trunks if it was divided, so that two worms, or more, replaced one. This was why it had been killed so often, yet reappeared. It had been reported travelling with a slithering pack of young ones, but these may have been only revitalised segments. The typed paper was held down with drawing-pins and appeared to continue somewhere else, on some not visible page, not presented for viewing.

BEING ENGLISH, the recourse they thought of was tea. There was a tea-room near the great house, in a converted stable at the back. There they stood silently side by side, clutching floral plastic trays spread with briar roses, and purchased scones, superior raspberry jam in tiny jam jars, little plastic tubs of clotted cream. "You couldn't get cream or real jam in the war," said Primrose in an undertone as they found a corner table. She said wartime rationing had made her permanently greedy, and thin Penny agreed, it had, clotted cream was still a treat.

They watched each other warily, offering bland snippets of autobiography in politely hushed voices. Primrose thought Penny looked gaunt, and Penny thought Primrose looked raddled. They established the skein of coincidences—dead fathers, unmarried status, child-caring professions, recently dead mothers. Circling like beaters, they approached the covert thing in the forest. They discussed the great house, politely. Primrose admired the quality of the carpets. Penny said it was nice to see the old pictures back on the wall. Primrose said, funny really, that there was all that history, but no sign that they, the children, that was, had ever been there. Penny said no, the story of the family was there, and the wounded soldiers, but not them, they were perhaps too insignificant. Too little, said Primrose, nodding agreement, not quite sure what she meant by too little. Funny, said Penny, that they should meet each other next to that book, with that picture. Creepy, said Primrose in a light, light cobweb voice, not looking at Penny. We saw that thing. When we went in the forest.

Yes we did, said Penny. We saw it.

Did you ever wonder, asked Primrose, if we *really* saw it?

Never for a moment, said Penny. That is, I don't know what it was, but I've always been quite sure we saw it.

Does it change—do you remember all of it?

It was a horrible thing, and yes, I remember all of it, there isn't a bit of it I can manage to forget. Though I forget all sorts of things, said Penny, in a thin voice, a vanishing voice.

And have you ever told anyone of it, spoken of it, asked Primrose more urgently, leaning forward, holding on to the table edge.

No, said Penny. She had not. She said, who would believe it, believe them?

That's what I thought, said Primrose. I didn't speak. But it stuck in my mind like a tapeworm in your gut. I think it did me no good.

It did me no good either, said Penny. No good at all. I've thought about it, she said to the ageing woman opposite, whose face quivered under her dyed goldilocks. I think, I think there are things that are real—more real than we are—but mostly we don't cross their paths, or they don't cross ours. Maybe at very bad times we get into their world, or notice what they are doing in ours.

Primrose nodded energetically. She looked as though sharing was solace, and Penny, to whom it was not solace, grimaced with pain.

"Sometimes I think that thing finished me off," said Penny to Primrose, a child's voice rising in a woman's gullet, arousing a little girl's scared smile which wasn't a smile on Primrose's face. Primrose said:

"It did finish *her* off, that little one, didn't it? She got into its path, didn't she? And when it had gone by—she wasn't anywhere," said Primrose. "That was how it was?"

"Nobody ever asked where she was, or looked for her," said Penny.

"I wondered if we'd made her up," said Primrose. "But I didn't, we didn't."

"Her name was Alys."

"With a *y*."

There had been a mess, a disgusting mess, they remembered, but no particular sign of anything that might have been, or been part of, or belonged to, a persistent little girl called Alys.

Primrose shrugged voluptuously, let out a gale of a sigh, and rearranged her flesh in her clothes.

"Well, we know we're not mad, anyway," she said. "We've got into a mystery, but we didn't make it up. It wasn't a delusion. So it was good we met, because now we needn't be afraid we're mad, need we, we can get on with things, so to speak?"

THEY ARRANGED to have dinner together the following evening. They were staying in different bed-and-breakfasts and neither of them thought of exchanging addresses. They agreed on a restaurant in the market square of the local town—*Seraphina's Hot Pot*—and a time, seven-thirty. They did not even discuss spending the next day together. Primrose went on a local bus tour. Penny asked for sandwiches, and took a long solitary walk. The weather was grey, spitting fine rain. Both arrived at their lodgings with headaches, and both made tea with the teabags and kettle provided in their rooms. They sat on their beds. Penny's bed had a quilt with blowsy cabbage roses. Primrose's had a black-and-white checked gingham duvet. They turned on their televisions, watched the same game show, listened to the inordinate jolly laughter. Penny washed herself rather fiercely in her tiny bathroom: Primrose slowly changed her underwear, and put on fresh tights. Between bathroom and wardrobe Penny saw the air in the room fill with a kind of grey smoke. Rummaging in a suitcase for a clean blouse, Primrose felt giddy, as though the carpet was swirling. What would they say to each other, they asked themselves, and sat down, heavy and winded, on the edges of their single beds. Why? Primrose's mind said, scurrying, and Why? Penny asked herself starkly. Primrose put down her blouse and turned up the television. Penny managed to walk as far as the window. She had a view with a romantic bit of moorland, rising to a height that cut off the sky. Evening had caught her: the earth was black: the house-lights trickled feebly into gloom.

Seven-thirty came and went, and neither woman moved. Both, indistinctly, imagined the other waiting at a table, watching a door open and shut. Neither moved. What could they have said, they asked themselves, but only perfunctorily. They were used to not asking too much, they had had practice.

THE NEXT DAY they both thought very hard, but indirectly, about the wood. It was a spring day, a good day for woods, and yesterday's rain-clouds had been succeeded by clear sunlight, with a light movement of air and a very faint warmth. Penny thought about the wood, put on her walking-shoes, and set off obliquely in the opposite direction. Primrose was not given to ratiocination. She sat over her breakfast, which was English and ample, bacon and mushrooms, toast and honey, and let her feelings about the wood run over her skin, pricking and twitching. The wood, the real and imagined wood—both before and after she had entered it with Penny—had always been simultaneously a source of attraction and a source of discomfort, shading into terror. The light in woods was more golden and more darkly shadowed than any light on city terraces, including the glare of bombardment. The gold and the shadows were intertwined, a promise of liveliness. What they had seen had been shapeless and stinking, but the wood persisted.

So without speaking to herself a sentence in her

head—"I shall go there"—Primrose decided by settling her stomach, setting her knees, and slightly
clenching her fists, that she would go there. And
she went straight there, full of warm food, arriving as
the morning brightened with the first bus-load of
tourists, and giving them the slip, to take the path they
had once taken, across the lawn and through the
wicket-gate.

The wood was much the same, but denser and
more inviting in its new greenness. Primrose's body
decided to set off in a rather different direction from
the one the little girls had taken. New bracken was
uncoiling with snaky force. Yesterday's rain still glittered on limp new hazel leaves and threads of gos-
samer. Small feathered throats above her, and in the
depths beyond, whistled and trilled with enchanting
territorial aggression and male self-assertion, which
were to Primrose simply the chorus. She heard a cackle
and saw a flash of the loveliest flesh-pink, in feathers,
and a blue gleam. She was not good at identifying
birds. She could do "a robin"—one hopped from
branch to branch—"a black bird" which shone like
jet, and "a tit" which did acrobatics, soft, blue and yellow, a tiny scrap of fierce life. She went steadily on,
always distracted by shines and gleams in her eye-
corner. She found a mossy bank, on which she found
posies of primroses, which she recognised and took
vaguely, in the warmth of her heart labouring in her
chest, as a good sign, a personal sign. She picked a few,

stroked their pale petals, buried her nose in them, smelled the thin, clear honey-smell of them, spring honey without the buzz of summer. She was better at flowers than birds, because there had been *Flower Fairies* in the school bookshelves when she was little, with the flowers painted accurately, wood-sorrel and stitchwort, pimpernel and honeysuckle, flowers she had never seen, accompanied by truly pretty human creatures, all children, from babies to girls and boys, clothed in the blues and golds, russets and purples of the flowers and fruits, walking, dancing, delicate material imaginings of the essential lives of plants. And now as she wandered on, she saw and recognised them, windflower and bryony, self-heal and dead-nettle, and had—despite where she was—a lovely lapping sense of invisible—*just* invisible life swarming in the leaves and along the twigs, despite where she was, despite what she had not forgotten having seen there. She closed her eyes a fraction. The sunlight flickered and flickered. She saw glitter and spangling every-where. She saw drifts of intense blue, further in, and between the tree-trunks, with the light running over them.

She stopped. She did not like the sound of her own toiling breath. She was not very fit. She saw, then, a whisking in the bracken, a twirl of fur, thin and flaming, quivering on a tree-trunk. She saw a squirrel, a red squirrel, watching her from a bough. She had to sit down, as she remembered her mother. She sat on a hummock of grass, rather heavily. She remembered them all, Nutkin and Moldywarp, Brock and Sleepy Dormouse, Natty Newt and Ferdy Frog. Her mother didn't tell stories and didn't open gates into imaginary worlds. But she had been good with her fingers. Every Christmas during the war, when toys, and indeed materials, were not to be had, Primrose had woken to find in her stocking a new stuffed creature, made from fur fabric with button eyes and horny claws, or, in the case of the amphibians, made from scraps of satin and taffeta. There had been an artistry to them. The stuffed squirrel was the essence of squirrel, the fox was watchful, the newt was slithery. They did not wear anthropomorphic jackets or caps, which made it easier to invest them with imaginary natures. She believed in Father Christmas, and the discovery that her mother had made the toys, the vanishing of magic, had been a breath-taking blow. She could not be grateful for the skill and the imagination, so uncharacteristic of her flirtatious mother. The creatures continued to accumulate. A spider, a Bambi. She told herself stories at night about a girl-woman, an enchantress in a fairy wood, loved and protected by an army of wise and gentle animals. She slept banked in by stuffed creatures, as the house in the blitz was banked in by inadequate sandbags.

Primrose registered the red squirrel as disappointing—stringier and more rat-like than its plump grey city cousins. But she knew it was rare and special, and when it took off from branch to branch, flicking its extended tail like a sail, gripping with its tiny hands, she set out to follow it as though it was a messenger. It would take her to the centre, she thought, she ought to get to the centre. It could easily have leaped out of sight, she thought, but it didn't. It lingered and sniffed and stared nervily, waiting for her. She pushed through brambles into denser greener shadows. Juices stained her skirts and skin. She began to tell herself a story about staunch Primrose, not giving up, making her way to "the centre." She had to have a reason for coming there, it was to do with getting to the centre. Her childhood stories had all been in the third person. "She was not afraid." "She faced up to the wild beasts. They cowered." She laddered her tights and muddied her shoes and breathed heavier. The squirrel stopped to clean its face. She crushed bluebells and saw the sinister hoods of arum lilies.

She had no idea where she was, or how far she had come, but she decided that the clearing where she found herself was the centre. The squirrel had stopped, and was running up and down a single tree. There was a sort of mossy mound which could almost have had a throne-like aspect, if you were being imaginative. So she sat on it. "She came to the centre and sat on the mossy chair."

Now what?

She had not forgotten what they had seen, the blank miserable face, the powerful claws, the raggle-

31

taggle train of accumulated decay. She had come neither to look for it nor to confront it, but she had come
because it was there. She had known all her life that
she, Primrose, had *really* been in a magic forest. She
knew that the forest was the source of terror. She had
never frightened the littl'uns she entertained at parties, in schools, in crèches, with tales of lost children in
forests. She frightened them with slimy things that
came up the plughole, or swarmed out of the U-bend
in the lavatory, or tapped on windows at night, and
were despatched by bravery and magic. There were
waiting hobgoblins in urban dumps beyond the street-
lights. But the woods in her tales were sources of glamour, of rich colours and unseen hidden life, flower
fairies and more magical beings. They were places
where you used words like spangles and sequins for
real dewdrops on real dock leaves. Primrose knew that
glamour and the thing they had seen came from the
same place, that brilliance and the ashen stink had the
same source. She made them safe for the littl'uns by
restricting them to pantomime flats and sweet illustra-
tions. She didn't look at what she knew, better not, but
she did know she knew, she recognised confusedly.

Now what?

She sat on the moss, and a voice in her head said, "I
want to go home." And she heard herself give a bitter,
entirely grown-up little laugh, for what was home?
What did she know about home?

Where she lived was above a Chinese takeaway. She

had a dangerous cupboard-corner she cooked in, a bed, a clothes-rail, an armchair deformed by generations of bottoms. She thought of this place in faded browns and beiges, seen through drifting coils of Chinese cooking-steam, scented with stewing pork and a bubbling chicken broth. Home was not real, as all the sturdy twigs and roots in the wood were real, it had neither primrose-honey nor spangles and sequins. The stuffed animals, or some of them, were piled on the bed and the carpet, their fur rubbed, their pristine stare gone from their scratched eyes. She thought about what one thought was *real,* sitting there on the moss-throne at the centre. When Mum had come in, snivelling, to say Dad was dead, she herself had been preoccupied with whether pudding would be tapioca or semolina, whether there would be jam, and subsequently, how ugly Mum's dripping nose looked, how she looked as though she was *putting it on.* She remembered the semolina and the rather nasty blackberry jam, the taste and the texture, to this day, so was that real, was that home? She had later invented a picture of a cloudy aquamarine sea under a gold sun in which a huge fountain of white curling water rose from a foundering ship. It was very beautiful but not real. She could not remember Dad. She could remember the Thing in the Forest, and she could remember Alys. The fact that the mossy tump had lovely colours—crimson and emerald, she said, maidenhairs, she named something at random—didn't mean she didn't remember the Thing. She remembered what Penny had said about "things that are more real than we are." She had met one. Here at the centre, the spout of water was more real than the semolina, because she was where such things reign. The word she found was "reign." She had understood something, and did not know what she had understood. She wanted badly to go home, and she wanted never to move. The light was lovely in the leaves. The squirrel flirted its tail and suddenly set off again, springing into the branches. The woman lumbered to her feet and licked the bramble-scratches on the back of her hands.

PENNY HAD SET OFF in what she supposed to be the opposite direction. She walked very steadily, keeping to hedgerows and field-edge paths, climbing the occasional stile. For the first part of the walk she kept her eyes on the ground, and her ears on her own trudging, as it disturbed stubble and pebbles. She slurred her feet over vetch and stitchwort, looking back over the crushed trail. She remembered the Thing. She remembered it clearly and daily. Why was she in this part of the world at all, if not to settle with it? But she walked away, noticing and not noticing that her path was deflected by fieldforms and the lie of the land into a snaking sickle-shape. As the day wore on, she settled into her stride and lifted her eyes, admiring the new corn in the furrows, a distant skylark. When she saw the wood on the horizon she knew it was the wood, although she was seeing it from an unfamiliar aspect, from where it appeared to be perched on a conical hillock, ridged as though it had been grasped and squeezed by coils of strength. The trees were tufted and tempting. It was almost dusk when she came there. The shadows were thickening, the dark places in the tumbled undergrowth were darkening. She mounted the slope, and went in over a suddenly discovered stile.

ONCE INSIDE, she moved cautiously, as though she was hunted or hunting. She stood stock-still, and snuffed the air for the remembered rottenness: she listened to the sounds of the trees and the creatures, trying to sift out a distant threshing and sliding. She smelled rottenness, but it was normal rottenness, leaves and stems mulching back into earth. She heard sounds. Not birdsong, for it was too late in the day, but the odd raucous warning croak, a crackle of something, a tremulous shiver of something else. She heard her own heartbeat in the thickening brown air.

She had wagered on freedom and walked away, and walking away had brought her here, as she had known it would. It was no use looking for familiar tree-trunks or tussocks. They had had a lifetime, her lifetime, to alter out of recognition.

She began to think she discerned dark tunnels in

the undergrowth, where something might have rolled and slid. Mashed seedlings, broken twigs and fronds, none of it very recent. There were things caught in the thorns, flimsy colourless shreds of damp wool or fur. She peered down the tunnels and noted where the scrapings hung thickest. She forced herself to go into the dark, stooping, occasionally crawling on hands and knees. The silence was heavy. She found things she remembered, threadworms of knitting wool, unravelled dishcloth cotton, clinging newsprint. She found odd sausage-shaped tubes of membrane, containing fragments of hair and bone and other inanimate stuffs. They were like monstrous owl-pellets, or the gut-shaped hair-balls vomited by cats. Penny went forwards, putting aside lashing briars and tough stems with careful fingers. It had been here, but how long ago? When she stopped, and sniffed the air, and listened, there was nothing but the drowsy wood.

Quite suddenly she came out at a place she remembered. The clearing was larger, the tree-trunks were thicker, but the fallen one behind which they had hidden still lay there. The place was almost the ghost of a camp. The trees round about were hung with threadbare pennants and streamers, like the scorched, hacked, threadbare banners in the chapel of the great house, with their brown stains of earth or blood. It had been here, it had never gone away.

Penny moved slowly and dreamily round, watching herself as you watch yourself in a dream, looking for things. She found a mock tortoiseshell hairslide, and a shoe-button with a metal shank. She found a bird-skeleton, quite fresh, bashed flat, with a few feathers glued to it. She found ambivalent shards and several teeth, of varying sizes and shapes. She found— spread around, half-hidden by roots, stained green but glinting white—a collection of small bones, finger-bones, tiny toes, a rib, and finally what might be a brain-pan and brow. She thought of putting them in her knapsack, and then thought she could not, and heaped them at the foot of a holly. She was not an anatomist. Some at least of the tiny bones might have been badger or fox.

She sat down on the earth, with her back against the fallen trunk. She thought that she should perhaps find something to dig a hole, to bury the little bones, but she didn't move. She thought, now I am watching myself as you do in a safe dream, but then, when I saw it, it was one of those appalling dreams, where you are inside, where you cannot get out. Except that it wasn't a dream.

IT WAS THE ENCOUNTER with the Thing that had led her to deal professionally in dreams. Something which resembled unreality had walked—had rolled, had wound itself, had *lumbered* into reality, and she had seen it. She had been the reading child, but after the sight of the Thing, she had not been able to inhabit the customary and charming unreality of books. She had become good at studying what could not be seen. She took an interest in the dead, who inhabited real history. She was drawn to the invisible forces which moved in molecules and caused them to coagulate or dissipate. She had become a psychotherapist "to be useful." That was not quite accurate or sufficient as an explanation. The corner of the blanket that covered the unthinkable had been turned back enough for her to catch sight of it. She was in its world. It was not by accident that she had come to specialise in severely autistic children, children who twittered, or banged, or stared, who sat damp and absent on Penny's official lap and told her no dreams, discussed no projects. The world they knew was a real world. Often Penny thought it was *the* real world, from which even their desperate parents were at least partly shielded. Somebody had to occupy themselves with the hopeless. Penny felt she could. Most people couldn't. She could.

All the leaves of the forest began slowly to quaver and then to clatter. Far away there was the sound of something heavy, and sluggish, stirring. Penny sat very still and expectant. She heard the old blind rumble, she sniffed the old stink. It came from no direction; it was on both sides; it was all around; as though the Thing encompassed the wood, or as though it travelled in multiple fragments, as it was described in the old text. It was dark now. What was visible had no distinct colour, only shades of ink and elephant.

Now, thought Penny, and just as suddenly as it had begun, the turmoil ceased. It was as though the Thing had turned away; she could feel the tremble of the wood recede and become still. Quite suddenly, over the tree-tops, a huge disc of white-gold mounted and hung, deepening shadows, silvering edges. Penny remembered her father, standing in the cold light of the full moon, and saying wryly that the bombers would likely come tonight, there was a brilliant, cloud-less full moon. He had vanished in an oven of red-yellow roaring, Penny had guessed, or been told, or imagined. Her mother had sent her away before allow-ing the fireman to speak, who had come with the news. She had been a creep-mouse on stairs and in cubby-holes, trying to overhear what was being imparted, to be given a fragment of reality with which to attach herself to the truth of her mother's pain. Her mother didn't, or couldn't, want her company. She caught odd phrases of talk—"nothing really to identify," "abso-lutely no doubt." He had been a tired gentle man with ash in his trouser turn-ups. There had been a funeral. Penny remembered thinking there was nothing, or next to nothing, in the coffin his fellow-firemen shoul-dered, it went up so lightly, it was so easy to set down on the crematorium slab.

They had been living behind the black-out any-way, but her mother went on living behind drawn cur-tains long after the war was over.

She remembered someone inviting her to tea, to cheer her up. There had been indoor fireworks, saved from before the war. Chinese, set off in saucers. There had been a small conical Vesuvius, with a blue touch-paper and a pink and grey dragon painted on. It had done nothing but sputter until they had almost stopped looking, and then it spewed a coil of fantastically light ash, that rose and rose, becoming five or six times as large as the original, and then abruptly was still. Like a grey bun, or a very old turd. She began to cry. It was ungrateful of her. An effort had been made, to which she had not responded.

The moon had released the wood, it seemed. Penny stood up and brushed leaf mould off her clothes. She had been ready for it and it had not come. She did not know if she had wanted to defy it, or to see that it was as she had darkly remembered it; she felt obscurely disappointed to be released from the wood. But she accepted her release and found her way back to the fields and her village along liquid trails of moonlight.

THE TWO WOMEN took the same train back to the city, but did not encounter each other until they got out. The passengers scurried and shuffled towards the exit, mostly heads down. Both women remembered how they had set out in the wartime dark, with their twig-legs and gas-masks. Both raised their heads as they neared the barrier, not in hope of being met, for they would not be, but automatically, to calculate where to go, and what to do. They saw each other's face in the cavernous gloom, two pale, recognisable rounds, far enough apart for speech, and even greetings, to be awkward. In the dimness they were reduced to similarity—dark eyeholes, set mouth. For a moment or two, they stood and simply stared. On that first occasion the station vault had been full of curling steam, and the air gritty with ash. Now, the blunt-nosed sleek diesel they had left was blue and gold under a layer of grime. They saw each other through that black imagined veil which grief, or pain, or despair hang over the visible world. They saw each other's face and thought of the unforgettable misery of the face they had seen in the forest. Each thought that the other was the witness, who made the thing certainly real, who prevented her from slipping into the comfort of believing she had imagined it, or made it up. So they stared at each other, blankly and desperately, without acknowledgement, then picked up their baggage, and turned away into the crowd.

PENNY FOUND that the black veil had somehow become part of her vision. She thought constantly about faces, her father's, her mother's—neither of which would hold their form in her mind's eye. Primrose's face, the hopeful little girl, the woman staring up at her from the glass case, staring at her conspiratorially over the clotted cream. The blonde infant Alys, an ingratiating sweet smile. The half-human face of the Thing. She tried, as though everything depended on it, to remember that face completely, and suffered over the detail of the dreadful droop of its mouth, the exact inanity of its blind squinneying. Present faces were blank discs, shadowed moons. Her patients came and went, children lost, or busy, or trapped behind their masks of vagueness or anxiety or over-excitement. She was increasingly unable to distinguish one from another. The face of the Thing hung in her brain, jealously soliciting her attention, distracting her from dailiness. She had gone back to its place, and had not seen it. She needed to see it. Why she needed it, was because it was more real than she was. It would have been better not even to have glimpsed it, but their paths had crossed. It had trampled on her life, had sucked out her marrow, without noticing who or what she was. She would go and face it. What else was there, she asked herself, and answered herself, nothing.

So she made her way back, sitting alone in the train as the fields streaked past, drowsing through a century-long night under the cabbage-rose quilt in the B&B. This time she went in the old way, from the house, through the garden-gate; she found the old trail quickly, her sharp eye picked up the trace of its detritus, and soon enough she was back in the clearing, where her cairn of tiny bones by the tree-trunk was undisturbed. She gave a little sigh, dropped to her knees, and then sat with her back to the rotting wood and silently called the Thing. Almost immediately she sensed its perturbation, saw the trouble in the branches, heard the lumbering, smelled its ancient smell. It was a greyish, unremarkable day. She closed her eyes briefly as the noise and movement grew stronger. When it came, she would look it in the face, she would see what it was. She clasped her hands loosely in her lap. Her nerves relaxed. Her blood slowed. She was ready.

PRIMROSE WAS in the shopping mall, putting out her circle of rainbow-coloured plastic chairs. She creaked as she bent over them. It was pouring with rain outside, but the mall was enclosed like a crystal palace in a casing of glass. The floor under the rainbow chairs was gleaming dappled marble. They were in front of a dimpling fountain, with lights shining up through the greenish water, making golden rings round the polished pebbles and wishing-coins that lay there. The little children collected round her: their mothers kissed them good-bye, told them to be good and quiet and listen to the nice lady. They had little transparent plastic cups of shining orange juice, and each had a biscuit in silver foil. They were all colours—black skin, brown skin, pink skin, freckled skin, pink jacket, yellow jacket, purple hood, scarlet hood. Some grinned and some whimpered, some wriggled, some were still. Primrose sat on the edge of the fountain. She had decided what to do. She smiled her best, most comfortable smile, and adjusted her golden locks. Listen to me, she told them, and I'll tell you something amazing, a story that's never been told before.

There were once two little girls who saw, or believed they saw, a thing in a forest . . .

Body Art

THERE WAS CUSTOMARY BANTER in the Gynae
Ward at St. Pantaleon's, about the race to bear the
Christmas Day baby. Damian Becket, making his
round after a sleepless night of blood and danger,
didn't join in. His newest patient was at the furthest
end of the cavernous ward, in the curtained-off sec-
tion reserved for those who had lost, or might lose,
their babies, and those whose babies were damaged or
threatened. Dr. Becket frowned a little as he strode
between the beds, not quite hearing the mewing and
gulping of the infants or the greetings of the women.
He was frowning, partly because his patient's new
baby, a scrap of skin and bone in an incubator in
Intensive Care, was not doing well. He was also frowning because he was so tired that he couldn't remember
his patient's name. He did not like to admit a fault.
The baby should be doing better. His brain should
respond to his need to identify people.

He did not notice the stepladder until he had
almost crashed into it. It was very tall, made of very

shiny aluminium, and was directly under a circular fluorescent light fitting. He stopped suddenly, didn't swear, felt sick because his reactions were slow, and stared upwards into the light, which blinded him. At the top of the ladder, perched precariously on tiptoe, was a figure in what seemed to be a haze of pale filmy garments. Its head was a ball of shiny white spikes. Dr. Becket said that the ladder was dangerous, and should be got out of the way. From the hands of the creature on top of it fluttered scarlet streamers, which glittered wetly in the too-much light. It emitted a ghostly tinkling. *What is going on?* asked Dr. Becket, staring grimly upwards.

The Staff Nurse said it was his idea, Dr. Becket's idea. It was one of the art students, said Nurse McKitterick. Who had given up time and materials to cheer the place up in an original way. Dr. Becket had suggested it to the Art-College liaison committee, such a clever idea. . . . Yes, yes, yes, said Dr. Becket, I see. It looks a little dangerous. His tired senses took in the fact that the ward beyond the ladder was criss-crossed with a rainbow of coloured strips of plastic, and strips of Indian-looking cloth spangled with mirror-glass. There were also brass bells and clusters of those eye-shaped beads that ward off the Evil Eye. They did lighten the darkness of the upper vaulting. They also emphasised it.

His patient, whose name, Yasmin Muller, was of course written on the end of her bed, was sobbing qui-

etly. She looked guilty when she opened her swollen
eyelids and saw Dr. Becket's severe young face staring down at her. She said she was sorry, and he said he
didn't see what she had to be sorry about. His fingers
were gentle. He said she was rather a mess but it
couldn't be helped and would improve. She asked after
her son. Dr. Becket said he was hanging in. He was
strong, in so far as anyone born so much too soon
could be strong. It is early days, said Dr. Becket, who
had concluded that exact truthfulness was almost
always the best path to take, though the quantity of
truth might vary. We can't tell yet what will happen,
he said gravely, reasonably, sensibly. She saw him in a
blur, for the first time really. A wiry man in his early
forties, with a close-cut cap of soft dark hair, slightly
bloodshot eyes and a white coat. She said, out of her
own drugged drowsiness, "You look as though you
should get some rest." And he frowned again, for he
did not like personal remarks, and he particularly did
not like to appear to be in need of anything.

On his way back he remembered the ladder, and
was about to side-step, when the whole rickety structure began to sway and then toppled. Damian Becket
put out a steady hand, directed the thing itself away
from the bed it threatened, and staggered back under
the full weight of the falling artist, whose head hit his
chest, whose skinny ankles were briefly flung over
his shoulder. He clutched; his arms were full of light,
light female flesh and bone, wound up in the rayon

and muslin harem trousers and tunic, embroidered in gold and silver. His nose was in baby-soft, silver-dyed, spun-glass spikes of hair. Lumpy things began to bounce on the floor. Bitten apples, a banana, a bent box of chocolates. The woman in the nearest bed laid claim, loudly, to these last. "*That's* where my chocolates went, I was looking all over, there was only a few left, I was blaming the cleaners." The person in Dr. Becket's arms had quite definitely lost consciousness. Her skin was cold and clammy; her breathing was irregular. There was not, of course, a spare bed to put her on, so he carried her along the ward, and out into the nurses' area, followed by his entourage. There he laid her carefully across the desk, felt her pulse, flicked up her eyelids. She seemed bloodless and anaemic. Skinny.

"Just a simple faint," he said, as she opened her eyes and took him in. "In need of a good meal, I'd say, whatever else."

She had a nice little pointed face, rendered grotesque, in his view, by gold studs and rings in pierced lips and nostrils. She was white like milled flour. She sat up and pulled her shapeless garments around her. "I'm so sorry," she said in a breathy voice. "I'm OK now. I hope nothing got broken."

"Mr. Becket saved the situation," said the Staff Nurse. "Did you slip?"

"I felt dizzy. I don't like heights."

"What were you doing up there in those impractical clothes, in that case?" asked Damian.

"It was a nice idea. To decorate the ward. I offered."

She sat, slightly hunched, on the edge of the desk, swinging white-stockinged feet in streamlined modern nubuck clogs, with high wedged soles, open at the back. They were a dull crimson, stained with splashes of paint, or glue. Damian Becket bit back a remark about the idiocy of climbing ladders in such footwear, and asked instead, "When did you last eat?"

"I don't really remember. I was late for here, so I just ran out."

"I was going to take myself to the canteen for brunch. Would you like to join me?"

The nurses had piled the pocketed fruit on the desk beside her. She did not look at it.

"OK," she said. "If you like."

THEY WENT DOWN to the basement canteen in a service lift, accompanied by two green-gowned theatre porters and a trolley. The artist shivered, possibly because she was cold, which she should have been, in those clothes. He said:

"I'm Damian Becket. And you?"

"I'm Daisy. Daisy Whimple."

They went into the canteen, which had moulded imitation wood plastic chairs, *circa* 1960, and some unexpected prints, bright abstracts full of movement, on pale green walls. There was the usual smell of cooking fat, and a clatter of steel teapots. She hesitated in the doorway, and her white face grew whiter. He told her she didn't look too good, found her a seat, and asked what he could bring her.

"Whatever. Well, preferably vegetables. I try to be a vegan."

He came back with an English breakfast for himself and a vegetarian pasta dish for her, with a tomato side-salad. The pasta was pinkish and grey-green corkscrews, covered with some kind of cheese sauce. She ate the tomato, and turned the fusilli over and over with her fork, in the aimless way of children trying to heap leftovers to make them look smaller. Damian Becket, having eaten two sausages, two rashers of bacon, a fried egg, a heap of fried potatoes and a spoonful of baked beans, felt more human and studied Daisy Whimple more carefully. Anaemic almost certainly, anorexic possibly. An odd limpness in the wrists. He couldn't really see her body in the furls of her clothing but he had held it in his arms, and it was young and tautly constructed. She had blue eyes and sky-blue painted lashes. Her veins in her thin arms were also very blue, as was a kind of traced tattoo like lacy flowers, that infested her lower arms like the evening mittens of Edwardian ladies. Her nails had been very neatly bitten.

"You should eat *something*. If you don't eat meat and things, you know, you in fact need to eat *more,* to keep up the protein."

"I'm sorry. It's nice of you. I feel sick, that's really the problem, with the ladder and all that."

Body Art

He asked her about herself. He was not good at this. He was a good doctor, but he had no skill at talking, no ease of manner, he didn't in fact *want* to know the details of other human lives, except in so far as he needed to know facts and histories in order to save those lives. He was unaware that his conventional good looks were to a certain extent a substitute for amiability. Even now, he was thinking, if she talked a bit, she might lose her nervous tension and be able to be hungry. He imagined her from inside her body. Her cramped little stomach.

She said she was a student at the Spice Merchants' College of Art. She had wanted to be a designer— well, it was all she had ever been any good at at school, her education had been—with a fleeting look up at his face—much interrupted, rather haphazard. But really she wanted to be an artist. She had taken part in one or two joint studio shows, with the people she worked with. Some people quite liked her stuff. Her voice trailed away. She said she'd seen the notice in the art college asking for volunteers to make things for the wards, and she thought it was a really nice idea. So she'd come. She was surprised there weren't more. More students there, that was.

"Please try to eat something. Would you prefer anything else—fruit, a roll and butter, some cake—"

"Everything seems to turn my stomach. I'll eat when I get back."

He asked where she lived.

"Oh well, like, I sleep on my boyfriend's studio

floor. Lots of us do that. There's lots of studio space in the old warehouses. Once they get done up of course they go for astronomic prices, the floor-space, but people like students and such get like temporary bases in the ones that aren't done up—or not done up yet—you can get nasty surprises, your feet go through the floors and that kind of thing. But it's OK, it's a roof, and a workspace."

She said, doubtfully, she'd better be going then. She was still forking over the fusilli. He remarked that they were nasty colours, unappetising really, fleshy and mouldy. This interested her. She reconsidered the pasta. You're right, she told him, it's meant to look appetising, tomato juice, spinach. It looks a bit disgusting. Dead, maybe. Lots of colours are sort of deathly. You have to be careful. He said he liked the brightness of her decorations. They were in keeping with the hospital's modern art collection. Had she seen that? She said she had seen some of it, and meant to get a look at the rest while she was on this project. She stood up to go. She looked as pale as ever, no hint of any kind of pink, either deathly or flushed with energy. He said he would walk her to the door. She said he didn't have to, she was fine. He said he was going home anyway.

They stopped in the new entrance lobby round the central stairwell. Stainless steel and glass doors and cubicles had been fitted incongruously into the late Victorian red brick. The brick was that very hot, peppery red of the Victorian Gothic. The brick walls were decorated with panels of encaustic tiles, depicting chillies and peppercorns, vanilla pods and tea-leaves, nutmegs and cloves. St. Pantaleon's stood in Pettifer Street, just where it joined Whittington Passage. It was in Wapping, not so far from Wapping Old Stairs. It had once been a workhouse, which had become the Spice Merchants' Lying-in Hospital to which was attached the Molly Pettifer Clinic for the Treatment of the Diseases of Women. It had become St. Pantaleon's when the new National Health Service refurbished it in 1948, adding prefabricated temporary buildings which still stood. Sir Eli Pettifer had been a surgeon who had worked with the East India Company and with the British Army in India and in other places. He had written a treatise on the medical uses of culinary spices, and had made a fortune, through judicious speculation in spice cargoes. His daughter, Molly, had been one of the first generation of qualified women doctors, many of whom were allowed to train because a need was perceived for their ministrations in the Empire. Like many of them, Molly had been carried away by typhoid, whilst practising obstetrics and general surgery in Calcutta. Pettifer had endowed the hospital for her, and persuaded the spice merchants to endow it more richly still. He had left it his huge Collection, mostly of medical instruments and curiosities, with the injunction that it be made available for the instruction and amazement of the general public. It

occupied several locked strong-rooms in the basement, whilst much of it was still crated, and much
more heaped haphazardly in dusty display cabinets.
One of the paintings from the Collection—a Dutch
painting of an anatomy lesson being performed on a
stillborn infant—had hung in the entrance hall. It had
been Damian Becket's idea to take it down and put it
in the Hospital Committee Room, replacing it with a
large abstract print by Albert Irvine, which he himself
donated. Carried away by the brilliance of Irvine's
powerful brush-strokes, pink and gold, scarlet and
royal blue, woven with emerald and flicks of white, he
had talked the hospital into collecting other modern
works, inviting sponsors, talking the artists into loans
and concessions. Painted banners by Noel Forster
floated down from the inside of the Gothic tower.
Huge abstract visions of almost-vases and possible-
seashores by Alan Gouk, in bristly slicks of paint, purple, sulphur, puce, lime, ran along the walls. In the
corridors were Herons and Terry Frosts, Hodgkins and
Hoylands. A Paolozzi machine-man glittered, larger
than life, next to the reception pigeon-hole. There was
an Art Committee, who usually followed Damian's
suggestions. They had also put him in charge of the
Pettifer Collection, which he knew he should look at,
go into, catalogue, arrange, only he was so tired, and
there was so little money, and so many sick women,
and he preferred his abstract modernist brightness.
Indeed, "preferred" was too weak a word.

So he was a little put out when Daisy Whimple stared dutifully up at the banners, cast her eye over the brush-strokes and said unenthusiastically, "Yeah, very nice, very colourful. Pretty."

"What sort of work do you do?" asked Damian Becket levelly. "Not like this, I take it."

"Well, no, not like this at all. I'm into installations, or I would be if there was any space anywhere I could get to install anything."

"The things you are doing in the ward are—are bright."

"Yeah, I figured that was what was wanted. I mean, like, the notice actually used the words *cheer up* the wards, didn't it? I agree, really, you want easy cheerful art when you're in one of those places. Easy on the eye, yes. For *Christmas* and all that."

"But you haven't—installed—anything to do with Christmas. No snow, no Christmas tree, no reindeer. No crèche."

"No one asked for a crèche. I can't do that sort of stuff. It's all *kitsch*."

There was venom in the word. She added:

"And I don't suppose the establishment'd be too happy if I, like, *sent it up,* the angels and stars and stuff. Though the angels are the bit I don't mind."

He asked, on an impulse, which modern artists she really admired. The answer came quick, without time taken for reflection, as though it were part of a credo.

"Beuys. He was the greatest. He changed everything."

He was piqued to find that not much came into his mind, apropos of Beuys. He dredged.

"Didn't he work in fat and felt?"

She looked at him kindly. "Among other things. He worked with himself too. He sat for days and months on a stage with a coyote."

Damian said foolishly that you could hardly have a coyote in a hospital.

"I know that. I'm doing what was expected OK, OK?"

"OK."

He said that he would be very interested to see her work when she had finished it. He said he hoped she would get a proper meal. He said he was going to get a taxi home, and could he drop her anywhere. She said no, she needed fresh air. Thanks.

They parted. It was cold outside: an icy wind was blowing in off the Thames. It fluttered in her silly clothes, and ruffled her silver hair. He resisted an impulse to run after her and lend her his overcoat.

HE LIVED in a Docklands apartment, glass-walled and very modern, looking over at Canary Wharf. It was simultaneously austere and brilliant. His furniture was chrome and glass and black leather. His carpet was iron grey. His walls were white, and were hung with abstract works—several of Patrick Heron's 1970s silk-screens, some of Noel Forster's intricately interlaced ribbons of colour, resembling rose windows, a Hockney print of cylinders, cones and cubes, a framed poster of Matisse's *Snail*. He had also one or two brilliant Korean silk cushions in traditional green, gold, shocking pink and blue. He lived alone, since his parting from his wife, with whom he did not communicate. He considered himself hopelessly and helplessly married. He was a lapsed Catholic—this was something about himself that rose to the surface whenever—which was rarely—he was in a position where he was required to give a personal description of himself. He could have added adverbs—savagely lapsed, insistently lapsed, even in some sense devoutly lapsed. His way of life—including his attitude to his marriage—still ran furiously along the narrow channels cut by his upbringing.

His Northern Irish mother had meant him for the priesthood. He was to be her gift to God, she often said, having also decided that his elder brothers were to be teacher and republican politician, which they now were, showing, perhaps, the power of her gentle certainties. His father was himself a schoolteacher, specialising in Irish Literature, and had wanted Damian to be what he himself had not been, a true scholar, a linguist who spoke many tongues, a civilised man. Damian had tried to please both of them. They were kind and their tongues were golden. He had got as far as reading literature at University College Dublin, where he met his wife, Eleanor, who meant to be an actress, who had become since they parted a successful actress on the television. Eleanor was a good girl, and was tormented—in those distant days—by problems about contraception. She tormented Damian in turn, leaving him both over-excited and perpetually unsatisfied. They married, as a direct consequence, when she was eighteen and he was nineteen. Eleanor's sister Rosalie was seventeen, not scholarly, and not a good girl. She once got drunk at a party, at the height of Damian's time of over-excited frustration, and had suddenly stripped off her jumper and bra in a box-room where they were hunting for coats. She stood and stared at him, wild-eyed, wild-haired, laughing, and the great brown eyes of her large freckled breasts seemed to stare at him too. She told him not to be in a hurry. She told him her sister was a cold little fish, he hadn't the wit to see it because he didn't know enough women. He took her jumper and bra and made her put them back on. She went on laughing. A year later she was dead; she bled to death after a back-street abortion. In his dreams he still saw the spheres of her breasts, and the constellation of freckles, and the blind puckered brown eyes of her nipples.

He did not lose his faith as a consequence of her death. Nor as a consequence of its effect on Eleanor, who now wriggled away from his body as though he was going to damage or contaminate her. Nor out of any moral outrage—though he felt some—at the Church's interference in processes he wanted to believe were human and natural. (That included contraception. Human beings were not animals. They cared for children for perhaps a third of the normal human life. They needed to have the number of children they could decently and responsibly care for. Their sexual desires were unfortunately not periodic in the way of cows and bitches. Women were perpetually on heat unless, as in the case of his wife, the heat had been turned off. It followed that contraception was natural.) He lost his faith as a result of a vision.

The vision was conventional enough, in one sense. It was a vision of Christ on the Cross—not a heavenly appearance, but the result of an unnaturally close inspection of the carving that hung in his local church, a painted wooden carving, neither good nor bad, a mediocre *run-of-the-mill* carving of a human body, unpleasantly suspended from nails hammered through the palms of hands neither writhing in pain nor distorted by stress, but spread wide in blessing. He thought, The anatomy is bad, the weight would rip through muscle and sinew long before the man was dead. Some crucifixes did support the feet. This one did not. They were crossed, and improbably nailed through both ankles. Some care had been taken to depict the agony of the muscles of the torso, the arms and the thighs. The gash under the heart had realistic slipperiness where it opened; unreal immobilised paint-blood spilled from it, in runnels someone had taken pleasure in varying. There were no bloodstains on the loincloth, which carefully obscured the sex. The face was stylised. Long, unlined, with downcast eyelids, closed as in sleep, and a mouth slightly opened, showing no teeth. More artistic blood had been dribbled from the clutches of the crown of thorns in the abundant shaggy hair. The dead or dying flesh—the carving was *simply not good enough for him to be sure which*—was creamy in colour, with pink highlights. He thought, I belong to a religion which worships the form of a dead or dying man. He realised that he did not believe and never had believed, either that the man's bodily death had been reversed, or that he ascended into heaven, for there was no heaven, and all human descriptions of heaven made it pathetically clear that we can't imagine it well enough to make it at all attractive as a prospect. He would not meet poor Rosalie in any such place, and he did not think he would even want to. He did not believe that this one unpleasant death had in any way cancelled out the sins of the earth: Rosalie's wildness, the Church's obstructiveness and bloodymindedness, his grandfathers' deaths in bomb blasts in wartime (paternal) and peacetime (maternal). He *never had believed* any of it. He felt for the shape of the time—his whole life—when he would have said he believed, and was aghast to sense it like a great humming ice-box behind him, in which what he had been had kept its form, neither dead nor alive, suspended. He was a human bowed down under the weight of a man-sized ice-box.

He went on looking at the figure hanging by his hands, with outrage and then with pity. There was a man, who had been dying, and then dead. And there was an idea of who he was, which was a dream, which was a poem, which was a moral cage, which was a film over a clear vision of things. A man is his body, his body is a man.

From which it followed that Damian Becket, having straightened his back, and shaken the ice-box from his shoulders to melt he hoped, at the feet of the lifeless carving, had to concern himself with bodies. His vision had not taught him that everything was without meaning, that chaos reigned. There was order, but order was in time and space and the body. If a man—who had seen the ice-box—wanted to make sense of his life and live well, he must concern himself with the body. There were multifarious reasons why in his case it was the female body. His decision to become a medical student, at the age when he should have been about to earn his living, offended his mother and made his wife extremely angry. He was not quite sure why she was so very angry, and could not find out. Communication is much harder in intimate fear and anger than between casual companions. Silence spread into their lives. He went to London and she did not. She went to church, and he did not.

HE DISCOVERED COLOUR, at the same time as he took up the post at St. Pantaleon's. Every time he came home, he stared at the bright forms on his walls, and worshipped the absence of God in the material staining of paint and ink.

He saw Daisy Whimple several more times during his visits to the Gynae Ward in the days before Christmas. She seemed to be the only student who had chosen to work on that ward—the take-up of the hospital offer had indeed been rather disappointing. She had made several bouquets or bundles of odd things suspended from the ceiling—children's whirligigs, coloured feathers, plastic bubble-wrapping stitched with cut-up plastic beakers and bottles, green and blue. He could see her sitting cross-legged on the floor in the corner of the ward, wound in a coil of tape to which she was stitching plumage— hen-feathers, turkey-feathers, black feathers which shone like oil. He stopped once and asked her how all this was funded. She said oh, she had scrounged most of it. She said, if you look closely at a lot of these things—the little whirlies, the gauze flowers— you'll see that they're rejects, a bit torn. They look fine like this, if you don't examine them too closely. He said he would see she got reimbursed, all the same.

"I like doing it," she said. "It's my pleasure."

She said, "I'm putting the really colourful bits at the miserable end."

"The miserable end?"

"The no-hopers. The dead babies and tied-up-tubes end. Sodding rotten luck to have to lie there and listen to other people's kids squealing all night and not getting any sleep. I think you lot are cruel, if you want to know."

He said, "Beds are in short supply."

She said, with a return of the sudden venom that cut through her pale daffiness:

"I know all about that. All about that. The consultants are overworked, they have to have all their cases next to each other to get round, bad wombs next to good wombs and no-wombs mixed in. I do know about that."

"I'm sorry," he said. He wasn't a man for arguing. He walked onwards. The Sister said:

"She was in here last year, you know. Abortion with complications. Mr. Cuthbertson operated."

Mr. Cuthbertson had subsequently left, after several of his patients had been discovered to have been badly handled. Damian looked a question at the Sister.

"Raging infection of the tubes. Lost an ovary."

He did not want to appear to be prying, so dropped the question. He could look it up in the records. But there was no need for him to know the gynaecological history of Daisy Whimple, who was trailing paper garlands of sunflowers and pheasant feathers between the bed-heads of the no-hopers.

THE CHRISTMAS BABY was black twins, huge, healthy, and slow to deliver. Damian was there because there were complications, and because he liked to work on holy days and holidays. The ward, when they wheeled their patient in, was largely empty. The mothers and the no-mothers had Christmas cards on their lockers. Daisy Whimple's decorations spun and fluttered in the draught from the double doors. Daisy Whimple was sitting at the Sister's desk, eating a pot of strawberry yogurt. Damian said:

"I'm surprised to see you. You've made it all look lovely. But I thought you'd have gone home for the holiday, by now."

"Home?" said Daisy. "No, I haven't gone home." She looked at him rather bleakly. "You haven't gone home, either."

"I was needed—"

"I've made myself useful in a small way," said Daisy, looking at the Staff Nurse for confirmation. "Haven't I?"

"You've been great."

"I wasn't criticising. I was just asking."

He waited for her to say, "Well, you've asked, now sod off." But she just bent her fragile neck over the yogurt, and ended the conversation.

HE ASKED THE STAFF NURSE, when Daisy had left, what she thought Daisy lived on. Did she have a grant, or what? The Staff Nurse said she didn't know. She did seem to be coming in to get warm. "She hugs the radiators, when I'm not looking," said Nurse Ogunbiyi. "And she nicks things off the lockers and the trays going back to the kitchen. I gave her that yogurt. She talks nice enough, tells you little things, but she don't say where she lives at present, nor yet if she's got any cash."

ONCE OR TWICE, when the Christmas holidays were over, he thought he saw her flitting round the corners of corridors, or stepping into the lift. But he couldn't be sure. And he was tired, and she wasn't his business, his business was flesh, and its making, mending, and unmaking.

ON TWELFTH NIGHT the decorations were taken down by the hospital cleaners.

HE THOUGHT of Daisy Whimple again when the Hospital Art Collection Committee met in the board-room, under Sir Eli Pettifer's Dutch painting of the anatomy lesson. There stood the doctor, stretching out the taut umbilical cord in two fastidious fingers. There lay the dead child, its belly opened like a flower, still attached to the veined medusa-like mound, which had been part of its mother. There stood the black-robed Dutchmen, looking solemnly at the painter. There, oddly, was a small boy, aged perhaps ten, also black-robed, holding up the skeleton of a child of roughly the same size as the peaceful corpse under dissection. The skull smiled; skulls always do; it was the only smile in the serious painting. Martha Sharpin, who was early for the meeting, like Damian, said to him that it was historically interesting as to whether the skeletal child was a religious *memento mori* or simply an anatomical demonstration. She believed it must be religious, because of the odd age of the child who held it up. Damian said that as a lapsed Catholic he wanted to believe it was simply an elegant way of presenting anatomical facts. He had a horror, he said, of the musty world of relics and bits of skin and bone which ought no longer to have meaning if their ex-inhabitants were in heaven. Martha Sharpin said he was forgetting the resurrection of the body, for one thing. And for another, the stillborn were not in heaven but in limbo, forever unbaptised.

"Are you a Catholic?"

"No," said Martha Sharpin, "an art historian."

Martha represented the Spice Merchants' Foundation on the Committee. She was the Foundation's

Arts Co-ordinator, new to the job, having succeeded Letitia Holm, an elderly aesthete from the second generation of Bloomsbury. She was regarded, with approval, as "new blood" by the distinguished trustees of the Foundation, and also with suspicion, as very young, and possibly lacking gravitas. She had a Courtauld Ph.D.—her subject had been the *Vanitas* in seventeenth-century painting—and a subsequent qualification in arts administration. She was in her thirties, with smooth, dark, well-cut hair and a strong-featured bony face. Her skin was golden, possibly with a hint of the oriental. She had very black brows and lashes, and dark chocolate-brown eyes: she appeared to wear no make-up, and appeared to need none. She wore the usual well-cut black trouser suit, and a scarf made of some shimmering permanently pleated textile in silver-blue, pinned, with a large glass mosaic brooch, into a shape that resembled the stocks and neckties of the people in the painting. Damian Becket liked the look of her. This was the second time they had met, the second committee meeting they had both attended. She had decided he was the mover and shaker of this committee, and that she needed to get to know him. She said:

"I have to say, the installation in the entrance hall is marvellous. Makes you want to sing, which is hard, in a hospital. Letitia told me you were the one with the ideas."

"Letitia was very helpful to me about where to

buy things for myself. I buy prints. My very first was a print by Bert Irvin called *Magdalen.* We bought one for the second floor, too. Rushing coloured forms, with grey. I puzzled about why it was called Magdalen—being a lapsed Catholic. Irvin names his work quite arbitrarily for the roads round his studio. I like that. Grey road, rushing colours."

"You collect?"

"I wouldn't call it that. I buy prints. Tell me about Joseph Beuys."

The connection seemed odd to Martha, who raised her thick brows and opened her mouth, just as the rest of the committee came in. An almoner, a nursing supervisor, the bursar, a representative from the Art College, a junior lawyer from the Spice Merchants. The Art College representative was a performance artist whose attendance and attention at the meetings were both erratic. When he spoke, which was very infrequently, he spoke in sentences like unravelling knitting, with endless dependent clauses depending on dependent clauses ending in lacunae and stuttering. Letitia Holm had disliked and despised him. She said his conversation was like his art, which consisted of a kind of hopeless-Houdini self-suspension from anything upright—lamp-posts, railway bridges, river bridges—in cradles or bags of knotted ropes of all thicknesses. Damian did not know what Martha Sharpin thought of him. He needed to find out.

The meeting wound on. Damian reported the purchase of a painting by Thérèse Oulton and the gift by an anonymous donor of some prints by Tom Phillips. The nursing supervisor reported on the scheme for ward decoration by the art students. She said there had been problems with someone trying to bring unhygienic things into the ward with the incubators. And some of the students had started things and not come back, leaving bits of mistletoe and oranges with cloves, cluttering the Surgical Ward. Damian Becket said he thought the decoration of the Gynae Ward had been very successful, very imaginative and unusual. He thought they should thank Miss Whimple. He asked Joey Blount, the performance artist, if he knew Miss Whimple. Not personally, said Joey Blount. Not at all, actually.

The meeting always ended with the problem of Eli Pettifer's Collection, which was always deferred. It was a condition of the bequest—and of all Pettifer's other munificent bequests—that the Collection should be maintained and appropriately displayed. And there it was, in boxes, and old display cabinets you couldn't make your way between. Daunting. They'd once had a real cataloguer, said the Bursar, who had been in there for six months, and got very depressed by the dust and the darkness. She turned out to have catalogued *one box* when she left, according to a system no one could make head or tail of. Moreover, she'd developed a mystery virus, which she claimed must have come out of the boxes, and had threatened to sue the hospital.

Martha asked whether the Collection was labelled. Yes, said the Bursar, most of it had little hand-written stickers and tags. It was hard to know where to start, he said gloomily. Martha said she would like to see it. The Bursar said this was more than Letitia had offered to do. Letitia was squeamish. Martha said she herself was not, and would take a look at what was there. Damian said he would be happy to show her round.

So Damian Becket and Martha Sharpin made a clanking descent in the steel cage into the bowels of the hospital. The door to the Collection was opened by a coded keyboard: Damian punched in his code and pushed it open. Martha Sharpin exclaimed at the extent of it. There were several rooms, opening off a central one which had a little murky daylight from a thick glass window let into the pavement above, through which they could see the soles of passing feet. There were rooms within rooms, made of crates and packing-cases. There were cabinets along the walls of the rooms containing shelf after shelf of medical implements and curiosities. Martha walked along, staring in. Damian followed her. Shelf after shelf after shelf of syringes: cartridge syringes, laryngeal syringes, varicose vein syringes, haemorrhoid syringes, lachrymal syringes, exhausting syringes, made from ivory and ebony, brass and steel. From another cabinet shelf after shelf of glass eyes stared at them from neatly segmented boxes, or squinnied higgledy-piggledy, like collections of marbles. There were bottles—ancient

tear-bottles, ornate pharmacy bottles in pale rose with
gilded letters, preserving jars, specimen jars. There
were surgical and gynaecological implements, repeated,
repeated. Saws and vices, forceps and tweezers, stetho-
scopes, breast-pumps and urinary bottles. Shelves of
artificial nipples, lead and silver, rubber and bakelite.
Prostheses of all kinds, noses, ears, breasts, penises,
wooden hands, mechanical hands, wire feet, booted
feet, artificial buttocks, endless faded hair, in coils, in
tangles, in envelopes with the names of the dead men
and women from whom it had been clipped. There
were specimens also. Human brains and human tes-
ticles in jars of formaldehyde. Shelves of foetuses,
monkeys, armadillos, rats, sows, boys, girls and an elephant. Monsters also, humans and creatures born
with no head, or two heads, stunted arms or spare
fingers, conjoined twins and wizened hair-balls. One
case, which was arranged with some aesthetic inten-
tion, contained a series of nineteenth-century glass
ornamental domes—or maybe museum exhibits—
in which foetal skeletons were at play with wreaths
of dried flowers, wax grapes, skeleton leaves and
branches of dead coral. Others contained wax humans
divided vertically, fleshed and clothed on the left
hand, polished skeleton and skull on the right. Martha
lingered over these. She had seen similar things, but
never so many, never so strange. Damian pulled open
a tall crate from which woodshavings were emerging.
Inside was what looked like a white statue of a god-

dess, a young woman with closed eyes and a curiously flaccid surface, folds of flesh rolling back towards her spine. He realised that she should be lying on her back, and saw that she was swollen to bursting, a full-term gravid woman. Then he bent to read the label, and saw that what he was seeing was the plaster cast made from the body of one Mercy Parker. He remembered that such plaster casts were made for teaching purposes. The deliquescent flesh was the other side of rigor mortis.

He closed her in again, and went back to Martha Sharpin, who was intent on a collection of small ivory women, some occidental, some oriental, each a few inches long, lying in various postures, curved for sleep, or extended. They all had removable, thimble-sized navel-and-stomach, which could display, and did, the miniature heart, lungs and intestines, or the curled foetus in the womb. Martha asked Damian if they were diagnostic or votive. He said he didn't know. He said, thinking of the lead nipples which must have poisoned what they were intended to purify, that the whole thing was a collection of attempts to preserve and lengthen life, which nevertheless bore witness to human interventions that had drastically shortened it. He pointed at the early gynaecological forceps.

"A huge step forward. But spreading puerperal fever wherever they were used. What am I going to do, Dr. Sharpin?"

"Martha, please. You need someone to make a

start on conservation advice and cataloguing. Someone brave, who won't get bogged down, and won't be slapdash."

"Do you know such a paragon?"

"No. But I could work on it—say one afternoon a week—myself, and get it into a state where it could be handed over to a proper curator."

Damian said he could think of no better solution. Martha said she would be glad if he could provide a dogsbody—someone to lift and dust, and help with labels.

The image of Daisy Whimple, a little inappropriately, visited Damian's mind.

"I know an art student. She did some good decorations in the Gynae Ward, for Christmas."

"She'd need to be able to spell. It's often not their strong point."

Damian had no idea whether Daisy could spell. Nor, when he asked in the ward, did any of the nurses know where she lived. Nor when, with unusual persistence for an overworked man, he called the Art College, could they enlighten him, though they promised to speak to her if she came in to classes, which, they said, she mostly didn't. Later, Damian wondered why he hadn't asked them for a competent student who could spell.

Martha Sharpin began her foray at the Collection. She only rarely saw Damian Becket. One day, when they met by pseudo-accident in the lift, she asked if his hours were regular enough for her to take him out to a meal, to talk over a project she had, to put artists in residence into hospitals. She thought he was the doctor who might see the point. Damian liked being asked out to dinner by this handsome sensible woman, who carried her knowledge lightly, and made life more interesting for many people. He found her attractive. He liked looking at women with good clothes, *on* their bodies, so to speak. He saw a lot of female flesh, slippery and sweating, even provocatively pouting and posturing at him. He liked the way Martha's sweaters moved easily around her waist—the sense that she was in control of herself. When they had their dinner, in a dockside restaurant overlooking the rolling grey mist on the Thames, and the snaking lights of the police launches, he admired her trouser suit, wine-coloured this time, fluid and well-cut, ornamented with another glass mosaic brooch in the shape of a paisley dangling an absurd pink pearl. He remarked on it. She said it was "an Andrew Logan. Called Goddess. It has tiny feathers embedded in it, look. Cosmic fertility."

They enjoyed their dinner. She explained the difficulties of placing artists in residence. They had had one once who wanted to photograph breast cancers, blow up the prints, and install them in the patients' waiting area. "They were spectacular photographs," she said, "but inappropriate. Or too *appropriating.* Photography has that quality. They weren't, so to speak, the artist's own cancers to display."

Damian said he supposed there was no sense placing an abstract colourist in a ward or a waiting-room. Martha asked if he'd found the art student he thought might help with the collection. What sort of work did she do?

"Well, the decorations were ingenious and colourful. I did get the impression she was so to speak slumming. She said she did installations. She mentioned Beuys."

"Ah, so that was why you suddenly asked about him—"

"I don't really know about him."

Martha said he was a great artist who dealt in dark things made of common materials.

"Fat and felt."

"Exactly. Usually on a large scale. Reliquaries of no religion. Things evoking wars and prison camps. He's probably the greatest single influence on art students today. They do *personal versions*—you know, the fish slice that my girlfriend didn't clean, the knickers I wore when I first kissed Joe Bloggs—the disk collection I pinched from my ex-lover—the purely personal. I am an artist so my relics *are art.* I'm not saying that's your student's line. She may really understand Beuys."

Damian said he had no idea what she did or didn't understand but he did know she was hungry. Anyway, he couldn't find her. They had better look for another dogsbody. And it didn't sound as though she'd be at all suitable for the placement.

THE NEXT DAY, out of the corner of his eye, he saw the white head and floating clothing whisk round the corner of a corridor. He strode on, making no sign that he had seen anything untoward, and suddenly turned back into the cupboard door she was standing inside.

"Hello. What are you doing here?"

The small face went through various thought processes without finding a suitable answer.

"I've been trying to find you. I've got a kind of a part-time job I thought might interest you."

"What kind of a job?" Suspicious, ready to run away.

"Can you spell?"

"As a matter of fact, yes. I was always a good speller. Either you are or you aren't. I am. I always get ten out of ten in those competitions for spelling things like harass and embarrass and sedentary and minuscule, I don't boast of it. It's like being double-jointed."

"Are you interested in work?"

"I'm an artist."

"I know. This is part-time work that would interest an artist." He wanted to say, a hungry artist, and smile at her, but he stopped himself. He saw her as a hungry child. She saw herself as a woman artist.

Body Art

Daisy and Martha were installed in the Collection. They put on white hospital overalls and white cotton gloves, and set about the discovery of the treasures and horrors. They worked Friday afternoons. When Damian was not working, he sometimes dropped in to see how they were progressing. All three exclaimed over a bottled foetus wearing bead necklaces around neck, wrists and ankles, or a large cardboard box that proved to contain the wax heads and hands of a group of nineteenth-century murderers, all looking remarkably cheerful. Damian took Martha out to dinner—to return the first invitation, and to discuss the artist in residence. They also discussed Daisy, quite naturally, and partly in this context.

Damian asked whether Martha thought Daisy could be the required artist. Martha said Daisy did not discuss her own work, and she, Martha, had no idea what it was like. Daisy was good at the conservation work—deft, quick-witted, with a good memory. "She says funny things about terrible things," said Martha. "But I feel she's sad. She says *nothing* personal. I don't know where she lives, or who she hangs out with. She seems to haunt the hospital."

"I think she scrounges. I think she doesn't get enough to eat. She's got a boyfriend. She says she lives on his studio floor."

"She intrigues you."

"She was in the Gynae Ward herself, last year. She had a bad time. I looked her up. It was a bad time that—that the hospital didn't exactly help—"

Martha said every woman must wonder what it felt like to be a man who saw so many women. In extreme situations.

Damian said his profession had made him unnaturally detached. I see them as lives and deaths, he told Martha, as problems and dangers, and sometimes as triumphs. Not mostly as people. I'm not good at people, said Damian Becket.

Martha smiled at him in the candle-light, and the lights on the river bobbed and swayed. She said:

"You're very kind, for a detached man."

"I'm kind *because* I'm detached. It's no trouble to be kind, if you remember to think of it. And I had a religious upbringing." He hesitated. He stared at the dark water. He said:

"It's odd what persists of a religious upbringing. I've no God and I don't want Him, I don't miss church and all the smells and singing. But I do somehow still consider myself married to my wife, though we haven't seen each other for four or five years now, and hope never to see each other again."

Martha understood very clearly that she was being offered something. She frowned, and then said:

"I've never had a religion, and never been married—never even come close—so I—have to use my imagination. Does your wife consider herself married?"

"She's an actress and a Catholic. That's a daft answer. Do you know, I don't know *what* she thinks."

ONE DAY, looking for Martha, he arrived to find the Collection in darkness and both women away. He began to wander amongst the shelves, when his foot squelched on something. He looked down. It was a potato chip and it was warm. He looked around and saw two more, at intervals. He bent down and touched them. They were both warm. He listened. He could hear his own breathing and what seemed like the sounds of the myriad dead things and outdated artefacts, shifting and settling. But he could hear breath, when he held his own, light breath, breath trying to be silent. He began to search the Collection, listening for a giveaway rustle, and heard nothing, except, breath, breath, silence, gasped breath, breath, silence. He stalked quietly, and between a long row of upright packing cases saw another potato chip, and what might be the opening of a burrow. So he peered into the darkness and took out the torch he always carried, and waved the pinpoint of light around in the mouth of the tunnel. Something white trembled vaguely at the other end.

"Don't be frightened," said Damian kindly. "Come out."

Louder breathing, more trembling. Damian went in, and illuminated a nest, made of white cellular blankets, the sort that are on hospital trolleys, old pillows. Daisy sat in the midst of them, oddly clothed in her white coat and gloves. A plastic box of chips nested in the folds of the blankets. Damian said, "If you eat those with those gloves on, you completely destroy the point of the gloves being sterile—"

Daisy sniffed.

"Are you *living* here?"

"It's temporary. I got kicked out of the studio."

"When?"

"Oh, *months* back. I sleep here and there. I sleep here when I can't find a floor to sleep on. I'm not doing any harm."

"You'd better come out. You could get arrested."

She scrambled out, a curious bundle of disparate garments, hospital white, vaguely Eastern underneath. She said:

"It's cold down here. It's hard to keep warm."

"It's designed to produce an ambient temperature for the Collection, not for squatters."

Daisy stood up and stared at him.

"I'll go then," she said, hopefully.

"Where? Where will you go?"

"I'll find somewhere."

"You'd better come back with me. And sleep in a bed, in a bedroom, if you can bear it."

"You don't have to sneer."

"Oh, *for God's sake,* I'm not sneering. Come on."

DAMIAN COOKED PASTA, whilst Daisy padded round his flat, studying his prints, with a slightly defiant, assessing look. He found he couldn't ask her what she thought of them. He didn't want to know what she thought of the floods of colour and delicate round harbours of his Herons, the lacquered reds, the gold and orange, the strange floating umber. He put food on the table, and kept the conversation going by asking her questions. He was uneasily aware that his questioning sounded very like a professional medical examination. And that she was answering him because she owed him for the food, the shelter, for not kicking her out of the job or out of the hospital. So he learned that she'd quarrelled with the boyfriend, after and probably because of the complicated abortion. He asked if she'd minded losing the baby, and she said it wasn't a baby, and there was no point in minding or not minding, was there? He asked her if she ate enough, and she said well, what did he *think,* and then recovered her good manners, and said grittily that a hospital was a good place for scrounging, you'd be surprised how much good food went to waste. He asked if she had a grant, or any other source of money than the work at the Collection, and she said no, she did washing-up in restaurants now and then—and office-cleaning. She said, economical with the information, that when she got her degree, if she got it, she might think of teaching, but of course that took time up that you might want to spend—need to spend—on your art.

He asked her what sort of work she made, and she said she couldn't say, really, not so he could imagine what it was like. Then she was silent altogether. So he turned on the television—his ex-wife flickered across the scene, playing Beckett and he changed channels quickly—they watched a football match, Liverpool against Arsenal, and drank a bottle of red wine between them.

In the small hours he heard his bedroom door open, and the pad of footsteps. He slept austerely in a narrow single bed. She came across the room in the dark, like a ghost. She was wearing white cotton panties—he had felt quite unable to offer her any garment to sleep in. She stood and looked down on him, and he looked more or less at the panties, through half-opened eyes. Then she pulled up the corner of the duvet and slid into the bed silently, her cold body pressed against his warm one. Much went through Damian Becket's half-drowsed mind. How he must not hurt her. Not offend her. She put cold fingers on his lips, and then on his sex, which stirred. He touched her, with a gynaecologist's fingers, gently and found the scars of the ovarectomy, a ring pierced into her navel, little breasts with rings in the left nipple. The piercing repelled him. He thought irrelevantly of the pierced hands of the run-of-the-mill man on the cross. She began, not inexpertly, to caress him. He was overcome by a wash of hot emotion—if he had had to name it, he would have called it pity. He took her in his arms, held her to him, made love to her. He felt her tighten and stiffen—thank God there were no more intimate studs or rings—and then she gave a little crow and settled with her head on his chest. He stroked the colourless fluff of her hair in the dark. He said:

"You're more a dandelion than a daisy."

"An old one then, a dead clock."

That threw him, for he thought of the dispersal of dandelion seeds and then of how inapposite this was to him and her with her ruined tubes. He said:

"You know, I have to say, all these studs and things, in soft body tissue—there's a considerable possibility they're carcinogenic."

"You can't worry about everything," said Daisy Whimple. "What a thing to say, at this particular moment."

"It's what I was thinking."

"Well, you could keep it to yourself for a better moment."

"I'm sorry."

"That's OK."

He lay on his back, and she lay curled on top of

him, and he waited for her to go away, which after a time, perhaps sensing the waiting, she did.

She stayed a week. She came to his bed every night. Every night he stroked the pierced and damaged body, every night he made love to her. At the end of the week she said she'd found a place to go, a friend had a spare sofa. She kissed him for the first time in the daylight, with her clothes on. He felt the cold metal of the ring in her lip. She said, "I expect you'll be glad to see the back of me. You like your own company, I can see that. But it's been good for you, what we did, for a little bit?"

"Very good."

"I never know if you mean what you say."

ONE RESULT of Daisy's brief habitation was that Damian allowed himself to know that he desired Martha. He wondered briefly if Daisy might have confided in Martha, and concluded that on balance, she would not. He went down to the Collection himself alone, and removed the blankets, the pillows, the food trays. He thought, in a week or so, when his flat was his own again, his sheets were laundered, his solitude with his images re-established, he would invite Martha there. She was a complicated person who needed slow, slow movements, he thought, not really sure why he thought these things. He too needed to move slowly, in a deliberate, considered way, he thought, putting behind him the vision of the white panties, the memory of the metal taste of the nipple-rings.

MARTHA'S BEHAVIOUR suggested she knew nothing either of Daisy's brief habitation of the Collection, or of the events in Damian's flat. Damian did not mention Daisy to Martha in any context. Martha said she thought she had found an artist in residence, a young woman called Sue Basuto.

"I think you'll like her work because it's elegant and colourful and kind of abstract. And I think she'd benefit from a hospital residence because she works with dripping water and pulses of light, in transparent boxes and tubes. She's part of a group show at the St. Catherine's Gallery in Wapping. Would you have time to come and look at it? We could perhaps go on and have supper or a drink if you'd like that."

Damian said he'd like that very much.

They had reached a point where they embraced decorously, cheek to cheek, on meeting and parting.

ST. CATHERINE'S GALLERY turned out to be a cavernous decommissioned red-brick Victorian church, perhaps ten years older than St. Pantaleon's Victorian buildings. Damian and Martha went to the opening together: most of the assembled company were art students, in tight black clothes, with pink or shocking blue hair. Their voices were small and shrill under the vaulting. They were given transparent plastic beakers of red Australian wine from a winebox, and potato crisps on plates.

Sue Basuto's work was just inside the door. It had a humming motor, and resembled an Escher woodcut of impossible flow patterns, tipping green floods into crimson funnels over shining slides which balanced finely and reversed the flows. Damian liked it but wondered if it was more than a toy. The people in the church were all gathered to stare at an installation on what had been the altar-steps, under the rood screen. It was hard to see, because of the crowding, and from a distance seemed like a termite heap, or carefully crafted rubbish tip.

Damian and Martha stayed where they were for some time, sipping the wine, which wasn't bad, asking each other whether Sue Basuto's work did or didn't have any reference to the circulation of blood and lymph in the human body. They decided to go and have supper and talk about it. They drifted over to the centre of excitement, before leaving.

IT WAS A REPRESENTATION of the goddess Kali, who was constructed like an Arcimboldo portrait out of many elements. She was enthroned in what resembled—what was—a seventeenth-century birthing chair, below which, under the hole into which the baby would drop, was a transparent plastic box full of a jumble of plaster Infants and plaster Mothers from crèches old and new. Kali's black body was a painted *écorché* sculpture. Her head was a waxwork *Vanitas,* half smiling lady, half grinning skull, lifesize, crowned with matted ropes of seemingly human hair. Her four arms were medical prostheses, wooden or gleaming mechanical artefacts, ending in sharp steel and blunt wooden fingers, and one hook, from which hung what looked like a real shrunken head, held by the hair. Her earrings were preserved foetuses, decked with beads, enclosed in mahogany-framed glass jars like hour-glasses. She brandished a surgical saw in another hand, and the final two arms were crocheting something in an immense tangle of crimson plastic cords. Her crochet hooks were the tools of the nineteenth-century obstetricians, midwives and abortionists; the dreadful formless knitting glittered like fresh blood. She wore, as she traditionally does, a necklace of tiny skulls—apes', rats', humans'—and a girdle of dead men's hands, in this case wax clasping plaster of Paris, clasping skeletal fingers clasping what looked like the real thing. Her legs were constructed of interlaced forceps and probes. Her feet were prosthetic—one booted, one a miracle of mechanical joints. She was signed, at her feet, with a flower-shape, a daisy, composed of a circle of the exquisite tiny ivory women round what, on inspection, could be seen to be a yellow contraceptive sponge, about as old as the church.

Damian went white with pure rage.

Martha said, "Oh, how terrible. And how *good.*"

Damian said, "Someone call the Police."

Martha said, "No, wait—"

The gallery manager, one of the black-clad thin women, came and said, "What's the problem?"

Daisy sidled up from behind the Kali, just as Damian began to say, very loudly, almost shouting, just controlled, that these objects were valuable museum artefacts—well, and body parts—they were relics and should be treated with respect, they were private property, and their display constituted *theft.* He demanded, he said, that the object be dismantled *immediately,* and the Police brought in.

Martha said to the gallery woman, "He's right. But for God's sake get photos of it before it goes. It's good."

"It's disgusting," said Damian. Daisy was standing indecisively, looking as though she was considering the possibility of creeping away through the vestry. He strode up to her and seized her bony little wrist.

"How dare you? How could you? We *trusted you—*"

"I wasn't stealing. I was borrowing."

"Rubbish. I suppose you would have sold it if you'd had an offer? I hope I never see you again."

Martha said, "Can't we—discuss . . . ?"

Damian roared, *"Get the Police!"*

The people slunk away. Daisy twisted free of Damian and began to tear down her structure. Damian shouted that she shouldn't touch the things without gloves, had she learned nothing, she was a little idiot, she seemed to be completely *stupid,* as well as deceitful and hypocritical and *disgusting . . .*

Martha put her arms round Daisy, who stood shuddering in her grasp for a few minutes, and then twisted free and ran out of the church.

DAMIAN'S DINNER with Martha did not go as he had planned. He was annoyed by Martha's readiness to praise Daisy's artwork. Martha said it showed real pain, a real sense of human harm, and threats to the female body. Damian said that the reason for this was simply the Things from the Collection, of which she had made an opportunistic use—a *parasitic* use. Damian shouted at Martha as though Martha was Daisy, about the desecration of other people's dead babies and body parts and suffering. Martha said she thought Damian had said that Daisy had lost a baby. That affected people. Damian said she had wanted to lose it, hadn't she, and for his part he didn't think that was why . . . And why does she haunt the hospital, Martha went on, inexorably. Because she scrounges, I told you, said Damian. Why was Martha so keen on defending a compulsive thief? I'm a woman, said Martha, vaguely and sadly. She had wanted him to notice that, this evening, she had dressed carefully, she had had her hair cut.

THE PRESS—luckily only the local Press—got hold of the story. "SHOCKING ARTWORK 'BOR-ROWED' FROM GRUESOME HOSPITAL REL-ICS." The hospital's overworked secretariat fended off queries with talk of a misunderstanding, said all was well that ended well, and said that when eventually the Collection was open to the public the public would see the true fascination and information value of the relics.

It was probably because of the Press stories that Dr. Nanjuwany, one of Damian's colleagues, thought of coming to see him. She was a young woman herself, good with patients, still a little nervous with medical difficulties.

"That young woman you were looking after—"

"I wasn't."

"The one who stole the Things from the Collection. She came to see me."

Damian closed his face into a simple polite listening.

"She wants an abortion. I looked at her records. She asked for one before, and we made a mess of her, because it turned out to be ectopic. She lost an ovary and most of the tubes. She says she was told she couldn't have any more children and I suspect she *was* told something of the kind. She worries me. She won't see a counsellor. I feel bad—since the pregnancy is a bit of a miracle—"

"I'll speak to her. Do you have an address?"

"Not really. We tried the one we had—which was the one she gave again when she filled in the forms— and they say she left months ago, they don't know where she is—"

"I want to know when her next appointment is."

If Dr. Nanjuwany was surprised, she hid it. "Thank you," she said, as though she meant it.

DAMIAN CREPT UP on Daisy as she sat in the usual long queue in the antenatal clinic.

"I want a word with you," he hissed, his face rigid with anger. She was sitting with the dandelion head bowed down, staring into her lap. She looked up at him whitely.

"No, thank you."

"It's not 'yes please' or 'no thank you,' Daisy, it's stand up *now* and come with me. *Now.*"

"You can't hit me."

"Don't be silly. I'm trying to help."

"That's not what you look like you're doing."

"That's because I'm also upset. I'm human. Now, come and talk this over, in private, come into my office."

SHE SAT THERE in his office, facing him, where all his patients sat. She said:

"I've done nothing wrong."

"Well, apart from theft, and unlawful entry, no. I want to talk to you about the baby."

"It's not a baby, right. It's a problem. It's got no future. We all know that, so just fuck off, OK?"

"Whose baby is it?"

"It's *not a baby*. The last one wasn't, it was a life-threatening *incubus,* that's what it was. Nearly killed me."

"Whose baby is it?"

"Whose do you think it is? That's all you men care about, nice potent sperm, sod the consequences—"

"Shut up, Daisy. If this is my baby—and it is a baby, it's a minor miracle—then I can't just let you destroy it—like that, without thinking."

"You don't know if I think or not. You don't know nothing about me. You can't call this a *relationship,* nobody ever pretended it was. It was a bit of fun and it went wrong. So I'm dealing with it in a grown-up way, a *responsible* way, to use Dr. Becket-think. It's not your body, it's nothing to do with you now. So get out of my life."

"It's my baby. It is my body. It's turning into my flesh and blood in there. You're not going to kill it."

"Very nice. And who will look after it, once it's got here, if it hasn't killed me and itself on the way?"

"I will, that's obvious. I'll support you—whilst you wait—and take the baby—and find a way to look after him. Or her."

"You would, wouldn't you? Shit. Get it adopted into a *nice* family, keep an eye on its progress . . ."

"It's my child. It should be with me. Fathers do love their children."

"Not unborn ones, in my experience. And I don't have no father, so I wouldn't know."

"They don't love unborn ones mostly because they don't imagine them. I deliver them all the time—especially those in trouble—so I do imagine them."

A generic howling newborn crossed his overactive mental imagery. He said:

"I'm sorry you have no father. Is he dead?"

"I just don't know who he is. I grew up in a commune. My mother was in a kind of East London ashram thing. All the men were meant to be fathers to all the kids. They weren't, not really. They all, like, went their own way and did their own thing after a year or two."

"So you lived with your mother?"

"No, she died. I lived a bit with my gran, but she went a bit crazy and got put into a place where they put crazy people, and I went to one of the other commune women, but she went to India, so I got fostered, like, with a teacher, which was the family I had, but I'm not in touch any more . . . Is this an interrogation?"

"No. I wanted to know. I don't mean to shout. I want my child to be born. If you can bear it."

"That's a joke."

"It wasn't meant to be. I can and will look after you—"

"No, but I like my own life, doing my own things my own way . . ."

"Daisy, please. It might be your only chance to have . . .

"Do you think I *don't know that?*"

HOSPITAL CONSULTANTS are used to getting their way. Daisy wriggled and argued. Damian simply heard her out and restated his position. She left, saying she would "think about it when you're not screaming at me." He said he would write her a cheque to buy food and Daisy enquired what good he thought *that* would do, since she had no bank account. So he emptied out the cash from his pockets, and put it into hers, as she sat there, sullen and silent. She said:

"This looks pretty disgusting. *I* think."

"You've got to eat. For two."

"That remains to be seen."

"Where are you living?"

"Here and there. Nowhere you could find me."

"Please. Promise to keep in touch. You will need looking after. Properly."

She said in a tired whisper:

"OK. I promise."

HE SAID NOTHING of this to Martha Sharpin. He was a doctor, he had taken the Hippocratic Oath, silence came easy to him. But what he was not saying inhibited him from saying anything else. He didn't call her. Then Martha, like Dr. Nanjuwany, knocked at his office door. They kissed, cool cheek to cool cheek.

"Damian, I've had a surprising visit. From Daisy."

"Oh?"

"She turned up very late last night and asked if she could sleep on my floor. So I said yes, and she came in, and just started crying—I've never seen anyone cry so much—and it all came out. Or a lot of it. She said you are insisting she doesn't have an abortion, and she wants an abortion, but she can't answer you back because you're so overbearing. And I wondered if a baby was in her interest—was possible for her—really. She's turned me into a kind of proxy mother. So I thought I'd come and ask you directly—since she's still on my sofa, and shows no sign of leaving—"

"The baby is in *my* interest," said Damian.

"But you are a *lapsed* Catholic, you said so."

"Seeing it's *my baby*—"

He saw, from Martha's face, that Daisy had for some reason been more discreet, or secretive, than he could possibly have hoped.

"Oh," said Martha. Damian said:

"I was trying to be kind. I was only trying to be kind."

He could not read Martha's expression. Shock, censure, disappointment, puzzlement.

"I found her camping out in the basement. I took her home. She got in my bed. It would have been

damnably *rude* somehow to kick her out, somehow.
You know. No, you don't."

"Oh, we've all gone to bed with people because it
would have been rude not to." A little too lightly. "So
now what?"

"Well. I—I shall take the baby. She needn't see it,
she clearly doesn't want it, but it must be *born*. I'm
responsible for it. What a mess."

They stared at each other. Damian, domineering
with Daisy, was hangdog with Martha. Martha said:

"She really is miserable. She's twisting about like an
octopus on a fish-hook. What about her—medical
problems? Will it be straightforward? She's scared
stiff."

"Possibly it won't. Won't be straightforward. I don't
know. There are very clear rights and wrongs in this
matter."

"Possibly there are, in your head," said Martha.

"You don't agree? You don't see—how I see it—
what I feel?"

"Not exactly. I'm an outsider. I see what she wants,
and I see what you want. The two don't fit very well."

There appeared to be no room at all for what
Martha herself might want, or have wanted.

"I need to find her somewhere to live—in a sensible way—or as near sensible as possible. Not your
sofa."

"Not my sofa. I'm not a saint and I have my own
life. I'll put my mind to the problem of lodging."

"I'll pay."

"Oh yes," said Martha. "I understand that."

A ROOM WAS FOUND, in a reasonable bed-and-breakfast, not far from where Martha lived, in London Fields. Martha helped in the search for the room and put a glass of freesias on the little dressing-table. She also helped Daisy to move in, in Damian's absence. She reported back to Damian that Daisy had said almost nothing, and didn't look well. She seems beaten down, said Martha to Damian. Defeated. She thought for a moment and added inexorably, "Terrified." Damian said frigidly that Martha was not to worry. It was his problem, and his decision, and he would see to it, and he was grateful for her help, and promised not to bother her any further. They looked at each other unhappily. Daisy now bulked large in both their minds; she had made them into the parents she didn't have, setting the kind mother against the domineering father, and herself against both. Life runs in very narrow stereotyped channels, until it is interrupted by accidents or visions. Daisy somehow impeded Damian and Martha from becoming lovers as a small child nightly interrupts its parents' embraces. Damian had this thought rather grimly as he drove to the hospital. He had the further thought that Daisy's real child— his child—when it was born, would be an even more effective impediment.

HE OVERSAW Daisy's pregnancy in a manner both cunning and draconian. He knew better than to invade her private life—or work life, whatever that was. But he checked what he knew about. He made sure she kept all her appointments, he monitored her monitoring, he checked the prescriptions, he interrogated Dr. Nanjuwany. He set his mind to thinking what to do with a baby. He did not consult Martha, he did not consult Dr. Nanjuwany. He did have a conversation with the hospital almoner, about what the legal processes were in the case of babies that were to be given up for adoption. This area turned out to be murky and fraught with difficulty. He listened to the almoner about the rights of the mother, the lack of rights of the father, about adoption procedures for a putative father who wanted an unwanted child. The simplest would be to marry, said the almoner. Not possible, said Damian. Damian, naturally law-abiding, and troubled about the legal status of his unborn child, nevertheless decided by default simply to do what was best and sort out a *de facto* situation later. He found out about nanny agencies.

HE WAS SUBJECTED, over the remaining months of gestation, to a kind of martyrdom by whispering.

Everyone "knew" what was going on, and since neither Damian, nor, surprisingly, Daisy, confided in
anyone, guesswork and innuendo flourished and tangled. Daisy did go so far as to report stonily that she
didn't want the baby, and didn't want to be told how it
was getting on, she wasn't keeping it, it was all someone else's business, thank you. Damian was present
when the first ultrasound pictures of the child, stirring
in its fluid bath, appeared on the screen. Daisy turned
her face away. Dr. Nanjuwany said, "Do you want
to know the sex or not? Some people like to be
surprised."

Damian said, "It's a girl. I can see her. She's fine."

Daisy said, "You, Dr. Becket, will you *go away*,
please."

HE INTERVIEWED NANNIES. They came and sat
on his sofa in his elegant flat, and stared at his paintings. He told them that the newborn baby would
arrive in three months, and that it was his own baby
whose mother would be unable to care for her. They
stared with a child-carer's pity at the pale upholstery.
One, who was friendly, and the eldest of seven—"I've
looked after kids since I was twelve years old, I know
all their ways . . ."—he rejected because she was Irish,
and wore a religious medal. One, very upper-class, had
a slightly loopy look and said she didn't think Docklands was a very suitable place to bring up a baby.

They need fresh air, she said, looking as though finding even these words was a disagreeable effort to her. He didn't like the sensation of being about to be dependent on, in need of placating, these unknown young women. He finally picked a Dane, called Astrid, largely because she knew about painting, exclaimed over the Herons and the Terry Frosts, said, without pushing, that it would be good for a child to grow up amidst such colour.

DAISY NEARLY LOST the baby at seven months. She was in the hospital for a week, with symptoms of pre-eclampsia, curious pillows of swollen flesh growing around her stick-like ankles. Damian visited her every day. He checked up on her body, and his child's body inside her body. She didn't really talk to him any more. The defiance had gone out of her, and was replaced by an unnerving combination of resignation and fear. When Damian said the foetus was in a good position, or that her blood-pressure had improved, she said, "Well, that's good, then," as though she expected nothing, either good or bad.

If Martha visited Daisy, Damian didn't see her. He had seen Martha drive away from the hospital with a man—a man in a good mohair suit, with longish hair, talking animatedly. Martha had her own life. He had a wife in Ireland and an unborn baby in Pondicherry Ward.

Bᴜᴛ ɪᴛ ᴡᴀꜱ to Martha that Daisy ran when her waters broke, unexpectedly early. Martha, mistrustful of ambulances, put Daisy in her own car and drove her to St. Pantaleon's. Daisy, her body heaving, her face blue-white, said, "Don't go away, please don't go away." The admissions desk alerted Dr. Nanjuwany, who took it on herself to alert Damian. He came down to find Daisy clutching Martha's clothes, saying, "Don't go away. Please don't go away." Martha looked at Damian. She thought there must be some ethical reason why he should not be involved in what was about to happen. She observed that he was at the end of some tether, his self-control exaggerated absurdly. She said, "No, I won't go away. I want to see this baby."

Daisy said, "There won't be no baby. It will all go wrong. I've known that all along." She howled, very loudly, over a wave of contraction and pain, "It's going to die and so am I and *he* knows it is, and he knows I am, *he* knows . . ."

Martha said to Damian, as Daisy was wheeled away:

"She's in pain. She doesn't mean what she says—"

"Yes, she does."

"They say women in labour shout out all sorts of things . . ."

"They do. I know, it's my job. But she does think she's going to die. I see it now. I didn't see it before.

She's the sort of person I can't—I can't imagine what she really thinks or feels—*at all.*"

"Would it be all right if I stay?"

"It isn't your problem."

"She came to me."

He wanted to cry, *I* didn't. Exactly because she did I couldn't. And can't. He flipped his mind back to obstetrics.

"I need to check how she's doing," he said.

Daisy's labour was long and horrible. She made it worse by letting loose nine months of pent-in terror and rage, screaming, weeping, and tensing all her muscles. She could not be too much anaesthetised, for fear of harming the baby, whose heartbeat was irregular, whose presentation turned out to be very awkward, with a twisted shoulder. Dr. Nanjuwany in turn panicked, and, ignoring what she knew and had not been told were all the ethical reasons for not involving Damian, she turned to him. He ended up delivering a live baby, slowly, deliberately, skilfully, not because he was its father, but because he was the man at that moment in that hospital who could deal with such a problem. He stitched the dangerous rip in the neck of Daisy's womb, stroked the pale hair away from the sodden forehead, took her pulse, and wondered where her wandering soul was drifting as she relaxed into a drugged and unencumbered peace. He had nearly killed her. That was the truth of it.

HE WENT TO LOOK at his daughter.

She had been washed, and swaddled, and was breathing lightly, regularly. She had soft dark hair. She was a little bruised. She opened hazy mussel-dark eyes, and seemed to consider him. He looked back at her, not in pride at his achievement—although in the melodramatic way of real lives, he had saved her, and indeed Daisy. He was overcome with dreadful love and grief. She was a person. She had not been there, and now she was there, and she was the person he loved. It was simple and he was a changed man. His eyes were hot with tears. The hospital rustled and whispered behind him.

WHEN HE WENT to visit the next day, he found he was in the grip of an exalted fear. He was going to see the child again—that was the essential thing. In his mind he had named her Kate. He was going to see Daisy, who did not want to know or see Kate. He thought he would start with the difficult thing— he was not a procrastinator—the difficult thing was Daisy. Then he would revisit his daughter.

DAISY WAS in a curtained-off space of her own, with a bowl of fruit on her locker. She was sitting up in bed in a hospital nightshirt, and her hair was washed and floating. She was holding—he saw her—the baby, in her arms, at her breast. The baby was feeding. He could see the little ripples of movement in the fine skin over the back of her skull. She was feeding from the pierced nipple. Daisy's little face was completely wet with tears. Her little hands, with their tattooed mittens, tightened round Kate, and grasped. She stared at Damian as though he meant to rip the child out of her arms. Her lip, with its silly studs, trembled.

Damian sat down heavily on the visitor's chair. Daisy said, in a small but perfectly grown-up voice:

"I didn't understand. I didn't know. She's perfect. No, it isn't that, everybody says that. She's *somebody*, she's a person, and she's mine and she—seems to need me. I mean, it does seem to be *me* she needs. I mean, I can't help it, she can't help it, I'm—hers, I mean, I'm her mother." The word obviously gave her trouble. She repeated, "I didn't understand. I didn't know."

Damian said, "You are right of course. She is also mine." He could have added "And I am hers," but he wasn't capable of so much rhetoric.

"You know, they all go on about love. Love, love, love. You and me, me and you—well, not you and me *personally*, but in the abstract. No one writes songs to babies, do they? But when I *saw* her—that was love, that was *it*, I know what it is—"

"I know. That's what I felt. When I saw her."

The baby hiccupped. Awkwardly, but gently, Daisy

tipped her up on her shoulder and patted her back. Then, gingerly, she held her out to Damian, who took her in his arms, and looked down into the unique, lovely face.

"What the hell are we going to do now?" Damian asked.

Martha, bringing a posy of daisies and anemones, came into the little space to find them both staring at the child, who lay on her shawl on the bed between them. Damian and Daisy had faces of baffled adoration. Daisy was still weeping, steadily and easily. It was perfectly clear to Martha what had happened. She thought of walking away, quickly. Damian repeated, just as he caught sight of Martha:

"What the hell are we going to do now?"

Daisy said to Martha like a child to its mother:

"I didn't understand. I didn't know."

"Don't cry," said Martha, coming further in. She saw that Damian had tears in his eyes. The baby began to cry and Damian and Daisy both put out their arms to pick her up and comfort her, and both drew back together. Martha, not herself moved to adoration, could see no satisfactory way out of this state of affairs, which was supposed to be not her problem.

"We'll think of something. Because we shall have to," she said. The other two nodded vaguely. All three continued to stare at the baby.

A Stone Woman

(For Torfi Tulinius)

AT FIRST she did not think of stones. Grief made her insubstantial to herself; she felt herself flitting lightly from room to room, in the twilit apartment, like a moth. The apartment seemed constantly twilit, although it must, she knew, have gone through the usual sequences of sun and shadow over the days and weeks since her mother died. Her mother—a strong bright woman—had liked to live amongst shades of mole and dove. Her mother's hair had shone silver and ivory. Her eyes had faded from cornflower to forget-me-not. Ines found her dead one morning, her bloodless fingers resting on an open book, her parchment eyelids down, as though she dozed, a wry grimace on her fine lips, as though she had tasted something not quite nice. She quickly lost this transient lifelikeness, and became waxy and peaked. Ines, who had been the younger woman, became the old woman in an instant.

She busied herself with her dictionary work, and with tidying love away. She packed it into plastic sacks, creamy silks and floating lawns, velvet and muslin, lavender crêpe de Chine, beads of pearl and garnet. People had thought she was a dutiful daughter. They did not imagine, she thought, two intelligent women who understood each other easily, and loved each other. She drew the blinds because the light hurt her eyes. Her inner eye observed final things over and over. White face on white pillow amongst white hair. Colourless skin on lifeless fingers. Flesh of my flesh, flesh of her flesh. The efficient rage of consuming fire, the handfuls of fawn ash which she had scattered, as she had promised, in the hurrying foam of a Yorkshire beck.

She went through the motions, hoping to become accustomed to solitude and silence. Then one morning pain struck her like a sudden beak, tearing at her gut. She caught her breath and sat down, waiting for it to pass. It did not pass, but strengthened, blow on blow. She rolled on her bed, dishevelled and sweating. She heard the creature moaning. She tried to telephone the doctor, but the thing shrieked raucously into the mouthpiece, and this saved her, for they sent an ambulance, which took the screaming thing to a hospital, as it would not have taken a polite old woman. Later they told her she had had at most four hours to live. Her gut was twisted and gangrenous. She lay quietly in a hospital bed in a curtained room. She was numb and bandaged, and drifted in and out of blessed sleep.

The surgeon came and went, lifting her dressings, studying the sutures, prodding the walls of her belly with strong fingers, awakening sullen coils of pain somewhere in deep, yet less than moth-like on the surface. Ines was a courteous and shamefast woman. She did not want to see her own sliced skin and muscle.

She thanked him for her life, unable to summon up warmth in her voice. What was her life now, to thank anyone for? When he had gone, she lied to the nurses about the great pain she said she felt, so they would bring drugs, and the sensation of vanishing in soft smoke, which was almost pleasure.

The wound healed—very satisfactorily, they said. The anaesthetist came in to discuss what palliatives she might be allowed to take home with her. He said, "I expect you've noticed there's no sensation around the incision. That's quite normal. The nerves take time to join again, and some may not do so." He too touched the sewed-up lips of the hole, and she felt that she did not feel, and then felt the ghost of a thrill, like fine wires, shooting out across her skin. She still did not look at the scar. The anaesthetist said, "I see he managed to construct some sort of navel. People feel odd, we've found, if they haven't got a navel."

She murmured something. "Look," he said, "it's a work of art."

So she looked, since she would be going home, and would now have to attend to the thing herself.

The wound was livid and ridged and ran the length

of her white front, from under the ribs to the hidden places underneath her. Where she had been soft and flat, she was all plumpings and hollows, like an old cushion. And where her navel had been, like a button caught in a seam at an angle, was an asymmetric whorl with a little sill of skin. Ines thought of her lost navel, of the umbilical cord that had been a part of her and of her mother. Her face creased into sorrow; her eyes were hot with tears. The anaesthetist misinterpreted them, and assured her that it would all look much less angry and lumpy after a month or two, and if it did not, it could be easily dealt with by a good plastic surgeon. Ines thanked him, and closed her eyes. There was no one to see her, she said, it didn't matter what she looked like. The anaesthetist, who had chosen his profession because he didn't like people's feelings, and preferred silence to speech, offered her what she wanted, a painkiller. She drifted into gathered cloud as he closed the door.

THEIR FLAT, now her flat, was on the second floor of a nineteenth-century house in a narrow city square. The stairs were steep. The taxi-driver who brought her home left her, with her bag, on the doorstep. She toiled slowly upwards, resting her bag on the stairs, clinging to the banisters, aware of every bone in knee and ankle and wrist, and also of the paradox of pain in the gut and the strange numb casing of the surface skin. There was no need to hurry. She had time, and more time.

Inside the flat, she found herself preoccupied with time and dust. She had been a good cook—she thought of herself in the past tense—and had made delicious little meals for her mother and herself, light pea soups, sole with mushrooms, vanilla soufflés. Now she could make neither cooking nor eating last long enough to be interesting. She nibbled at cheese and crusts like a frugal mouse, and could not stay seated at her table but paced her room. The life had gone out of the furnishings and objects. The polish was dulled and she left it like that: she made her bed with one crumpled pull. She had a sense that the dust was thickening on everything.

She did what work she had to do, conscientiously. The problem was, that there was not enough of it. She worked as a part-time researcher for a major etymological dictionary, and in the past had been assiduous and inventive in suggesting new entries, new problems. Now, she answered those queries which were sent to her, and they did not at all fill up the huge cavern of space and time in which she floated and sank. She got up, and dressed herself carefully, as though she was "going out to work." She knew she must not let herself go, that was what she must not do. Then she walked about in the spinning dust and came to a standstill and stared out of the window, for minutes that seemed like hours, and hours that seemed like minutes. She liked to see the dark spread in the square, because then bedtime was not far away.

The day came when the dressings could, should, be dispensed with. She had been avoiding her body, simply wiping her face and under her arms with a damp face-cloth. She decided to have a bath. Their bath was old and deep and narrow, with imposing brass taps and a heavy coil of shower-hosing. There was a wide wooden bath-rack across it, which still held, she saw now, private things of her mother's—a loofah, a sponge, a pumice stone. Her mother had never needed help in the bathroom. She had made fragrant steam from rosewater in a blue bottle, she had used baby-talc, scented with witch-hazel. For some reason these things had escaped the post-mortem clearance. Ines thought of clearing them now, and then thought, what does it matter? She ran a deep lukewarm bath. The old plumbing clanked and shuddered. She hung her dressing-gown—grey flannel—on the door, and very carefully, feeling a little giddy, clutching the rim, climbed into the bath and let her bruised flesh down into the water.

The warmth was nice. A few tense sinews relaxed. Time went into one of its slow phases. She sat and stared at the things on the rack. Loofah, sponge, pumice. A fibrous tube, a soft mess of holes, a shaped grey stone. She considered the differences between the three, all essentially solids with holes in. The loofah was stringy and matted, the sponge was branching and vacuous, the pumice was riddled with needle-holes. She stared, feeling that she and they were weightless, floating and swelling in her giddiness. Biscuit-coloured, bleached khaki, shadow-grey. Colourless colours, shapeless shapes. She picked up the sponge, and squeezed cooling water over her bust, studying the random forms of droplets and tricklings. She did not like the sponge's touch; it was clammy and fleshy. The loofah and the sponge were the dried-out bodies, the skeletons, of living things. She picked up the pumice, a light stone tear, shaped to the palm of a hand, felt its paradoxical lightness, and dropped it into the water, where it floated. She did not know how long she sat there. The water cooled. She made a decision, to throw away the sponge. When she lifted herself, awkwardly, through the surface film, the pumice chinked against her flesh. It was an odd little sound, like a knock on metal. She put the pumice back on the rack, and touched her puckered wound with nervy fingers. Supposing something should be left in there? A clamp, a forceps, a needle? Not exactly looking she explored her reconstructed navel with a fingertip. She felt the absence of sensation and a certain glossy hardness where the healing was going on. She tapped, very softly, with her fingernail. She was not sure whether it was, or was not, a chink.

The next thing she noticed was a spangling of what seemed like glinting red dust, or ground glass, in the folds of her dressing-gown and her discarded underwear. It was a dull red, like dried blood, which does not have a sheen. It increased in quantity, rather than diminished, once she had noticed it. She observed tiny conical heaps of it, by skirting-boards, on the corners of Persian rugs—conical heaps, slightly depressed, like ant-hill castings or miniaturised volcanoes. At the same time she noticed that her underwear appeared to be catching threads, here and there, on the rough, numb expanse of the healing scars. She felt a kind of horror and shame in looking at herself spread with lumps and an artificial navel. As the phenomenon grew more pronounced, she explored the area tentatively with her fingertips, over the cotton of her knickers. Her stomach was without sensation. Her fingers felt whorls and ridges, even sharp edges. They disturbed the glassy dust, which came away with the cloth, and shone in its creases. Each day the bumps and sharpness, far from calming, became more pronounced. One evening, in the unlit twilight, she finally found the nerve to undress, and tuck in her chin to stare down at herself. What she saw was a raised shape, like a starfish, like the whirling arms of a nebula in the heavens. It was the colour—or *a* colour—of raw flesh, like an open whip-wound or knife-slash. It trembled, because she was trembling, but it was cold to the touch, cold and hard as glass or stone. From the star-arms the red dust wafted like glamour. She covered herself hastily, as though what was not seen might disappear.

The next day, it felt bigger. The day after, she looked again, in the half-light, and saw that the blemish was spreading. It had pushed out ruddy veins into the tired white flesh, threading sponge with crystal. It winked. It was many reds, from ochre to scarlet, from garnet to cinnabar. She was half-tempted to insert a fingernail under the veins and chip them off, and she could not.

She thought of it as "the blemish." She thought more and more about it, even when it was covered and out of sight. It extended itself—not evenly, but in fits and starts, around her waist, like a shingly girdle pushing down long fibrous fingers towards her groin, thrusting out cysts and gritty coruscations towards her pubic hair. There were puckered weals where flesh met what appeared to be stone. What *was* stone, what else was it?

One day she found a cluster of greenish-white crystals sprouting in her armpit. These she tried to prise away, and failed. They were attached deep within; they could be felt to be stirring stony roots under the skin surface, pulling the muscles. Jagged flakes of silica and nodes of basalt pushed her breasts upward and flourished under the fall of flesh, making her clothes crackle and rustle. Slowly, slowly, day by quick day, her torso was wrapped in a stony encrustation, like a corselet. She could feel that under the stones her compressed inwards were still fluid and soft, responsive to pain and pressure.

She was surprised at the fatalism with which she resigned herself to taking horrified glances at her transformation. It was as though, much of the time, her thoughts and feelings had slowed to stone-speed, nerveless and stolid. There were, increasingly, days when a new curiosity jostled the horror. One day, one of the blue veins on her inner thigh erupted into a line of rubious spinels, and she thought of jewels before she thought of pustules. They glittered as she moved. She saw that her stony casing was not static—points of rock salt and milky quartz thrust through glassy sheets of basalt, bubbles of sinter formed like tears between layers of hornblende. She learned the names of some of the stones when curiosity got the better of passive fear. The flat, a dictionary-maker's flat, was furnished with encyclopaedias of all sorts. She sat in the evening lamplight and read the lovely words: pyrolusite, ignimbrite, omphacite, uvarovite, glaucophane, schist, shale, gneiss, tuff.

Her inner thighs now chinked together when she moved. The first apparition of the stony crust outside her clothing was strange and beautiful. She observed its beginnings in the mirror one morning, brushing her hair—a necklace of veiled swellings above her collar-bone which broke slowly through the skin like eyes from closed lids, and became opal—fire opal, black opal, geyserite and hydrophane, full of watery light. She found herself preening at herself in her mirror. She wondered, fatalistically and drowsily, whether when she was all stone, she would cease to breathe, see and move. For the moment she had grown no more than a carapace. Her joints obeyed her, light went from retina to brain, her budded tongue tasted food that she still ate.

She dismissed, with no real hesitation, the idea of consulting the surgeon, or any other doctor. Her slowing mind had become trenchant, and she saw clearly that she would be an object of horror and fascination, to be shut away and experimented on. It was of course, theoretically, possible that she was greatly deluded, that the winking gemstones and heaped flakes of her new crust were feverish sparks of her anaesthetised brain and grieving spirit. But she didn't think so—she refuted herself as Dr. Johnson refuted Bishop Berkeley, by tapping on stone and hearing the scrape and chink of stone responding. No, what was happening was, it appeared, a unique transformation. She assumed it would end with the petrifaction of her vital functions. A moment would come when she wouldn't be able to see, or move, or feed herself (which might not matter). Her mother had not had to face death—she had told herself it was not yet, not for just now, not round the next corner. She herself was about to observe its approach in a new fantastic form. She thought of recording the transformations, the metamorphic folds, the ooze, the conchoidal fractures. Then when "they" found her, "they" would have a record of how she had become what she was. She would observe, unflinching.

But she continually put off the writing, partly

because she preferred standing to sitting at a desk, and partly because she could not fix the process in her mind clearly enough to make words of it. She stood in the light of the window morning and evening, and read the stony words in the geological handbooks. She stood by the mirror in the bathroom and tried to identify the components of her crust. They changed, she was almost sure, minute by minute. She had found a description of the pumice stone—"a pale grey frothy volcanic glass, part of a pyroclastic flow made of very hot particles; flattened pumice fragments are known as fiamme." She imagined her lungs full of vesicles like the frothy stone, becoming stone. She found traces of hot flows down her own flanks, over her own thighs. She went into her mother's bedroom, where there was a cheval glass, the only full-length mirror in the house.

At the end of a day's staring she would see a new shimmer of labradorite, six inches long and diamond-shaped, arrived imperceptibly almost between her buttocks where her gaze had not rested.

She saw dikes of dolerites, in graduated sills, now invading her inner arms. But it took weeks of patient watching before, by dint of glancing in rapid saccades, she surprised a bubble of rosy barite crystals, breaking through a vein of fluorspar, and opening into the form known as a desert rose, bunched with the ore flowers of blue john. Her metamorphosis obeyed no known laws of physics or chemistry: ultramafic black rocks and ghostly Iceland spar formed in succession, and clung together.

After some time, she noticed that her patient and stoical expectation of final inertia was not being fulfilled. As she grew stonier, she felt a desire to move, to be out of doors. She stood in the window and observed the weather. She found she wanted to go out, both on bright days, and even more in storms. One dark Sunday, when the midday sky was thick and grey as granite, when sullen thunder rumbled and the odd flash of lightning made human stomachs queasy, Ines was overcome with a need to be out in the weather. She put on wide trousers and a tunic, and over them a shapeless hooded raincoat. She pushed her knobby feet into fur boots, and her clay-pale hands, with their veins of azurmalachite, into sheepskin mittens, and set out down the stairs and into the street.

She had wondered how her tendons and musculature would function. She thought she could feel the roll of polished stone in stony cup as she moved her pelvis and hips, raised her knees, and swung her rigid arms. There was a delicious smoothness to these motions, a surprise after the accommodations she was used to making with the crumbling calcium of arthritic joints. She strode along, aimlessly at first, trying to get away from people. She noticed that her sense of smell had changed, and was sharper. She could smell the rain in the thick cloud-blanket. She could smell the carbon in the car-exhausts and the rainbow-coloured minerals in puddles of petrol. These scents were pleasurable. She came to the remains of a street market, and was assailed by the stink of organic decay, deliquescent fruit-mush, rotting cabbage, old burned oil on greasy newspapers and mashed fishbones. She strode past all this, retching a little, feeling acid bile churning in a stomach-sac made by now of what?

She came to a park—a tamed, urban park, with rose beds and rubbish bins, doggy-lavatories and a concrete fountain. She could hear the water on the cement with a new intricate music. The smell of a rain-squall blew away the wafting warmth of dog-shit. She put up her face and pulled off her hood. Her cheeks were beginning to sprout silicone flakes and dendrite fibres, but she only looked, she thought, like a lumpy old woman. There were droplets of alabaster and peridot clustering in her grey hair like the eggs of some mythic stony louse, but they could not yet be seen, except from close. She shook her hair free and turned her face up to the branches and the clouds as the rain began. Big drops splashed on her sharp nose; she licked them from stiffening lips between crystalline teeth, with a still-flexible tongue-tip, and tasted skywater, mineral and delicious. She stood there and let the thick streams of water run over her body and down inside her flimsy garments, streaking her carnelian nipples and adamantine wrists. The lightning came in sheets of metal sheen. The thunder crashed in the sky and the surface of the woman crackled and creaked in sympathy.

She thought, I need to find a place where I should stand, when I am completely solid, I should find a place *outside,* in the weather.

A Stone Woman

WHEN WOULD SHE BE, so to speak, dead? When her plump flesh heart stopped pumping the blue blood along the veins and arteries of her shifting shape? When the grey and clammy matter of her brain became limestone or graphite? When her brain-stem became a column of rutilated quartz? When her eyes became—what? She inclined to the belief that her watching eyes would be the last thing, even though fine threads on her nostrils still conveyed the scent of brass or coal to the primitive lobes at the base of the brain. The phrase came into her head: Those are pearls that were his eyes. A song of grief made fantastic by a sea-change. Would her eyes cloud over and become pearls? Pearls were interesting. They were a substance where the organic met the inorganic, like moss agate. Pearls were stones secreted by a living shellfish, per-fected inside the mother-of-pearl of its skeleton to protect its soft inward flesh from an irritant. She went to her mother's jewel-box, in search of a long string of freshwater pearls she had given her for her seventieth birthday. There they lay and glimmered; she took them out and wound them round her sparkling neck, streaked already with jet, opal, and jacinth zircon.

She had had the idea that the mineral world was a world of perfect, inanimate forms, with an unchanging mathematical order of crystals and molecules beneath its sprouts and flows and branches. She had thought, when she had started thinking, about her own transfiguration as something profoundly unnatural, a move from a world of warm change and decay to a world of cold permanence. But as she became mineral, and looked into the idea of minerals, she saw that there were reciprocities, both physical and figurative. There were whole ranges of rocks and stones which, like pearls, were formed from things which had once been living. Not only coal and fossils, petrified woods and biothermal limestones—oolitic and pisolitic limestones, formed round dead shells—but chalk itself which was mainly made up of micro-organisms, or cherts and flints, massive bedded forms made up of the skeletons of Radiolaria and diatoms. These were themselves once living stones—living marine organisms that spun and twirled around skeletons made of opal.

The minds of stone lovers had colonised stones as lichens cling to them with golden or grey-green florid stains. The human world of stones is caught in organic metaphors like flies in amber. Words came from flesh and hair and plants. Reniform, mammilated, botryoidal, dendrite, haematite. Carnelian is from carnal, from flesh. Serpentine and lizardite are stone reptiles; phyllite is leafy-green. The earth itself is made in part of bones, shells and diatoms. Ines was returning to it in a form quite different from her mother's fiery ash and bonemeal. She preferred the parts of her body that were now volcanic glasses, not bony chalk. Chabazite, from the Greek for hailstones, obsidian, which, like analcime and garnet, has the perfect icositetrahedral shape.

WHETHER OR NOT she became wholly inanimate, she must find a place to stand in the weather before she became immobile. She visited city squares, and stood experimentally by the rims of fountains, or in the entrances of grottoes. She had read of the hidden wildernesses of nineteenth-century graveyards, and it came to her that in such a place, amongst weeping angels and grieving cherubs, she might find a quiet resting-place. So she set out on foot, hooded and booted, with her new indefatigable rolling pace, marble joint in marble socket. It was a grey day, at the end of winter with specks between rain and snow spitting in the fitful wind. She strode in through a wrought-iron gate in a high wall.

What she saw was a flat stony city, house after house under the humped ripples of earth, marked by flat stones, standing stones, canted stones, fallen stones, soot-stained, dropping-stained, scum-stained, crumbled, carved, repeating, repeating. She walked along its silent pathways, past dripping yews and leafless birches and speckled laurels, looking for stone women. They stood there—or occasionally lay fallen there—on the rich earth. There were many of them, but they resembled each other with more than a family resemblance. There were the sweetly regretful lady angels, one arm pointing upwards, one turned down to scatter an arrested fall of stony flowers. There were the chubby child-angels, wearing simple embroidered stone tunics over chubby stone knees, also holding drooping flowers. Some busy monumental mason had turned them out to order, one after the other, their sweetly arched lips, or apple-cheeks, well-practised tricks of the trade. There was no other living person in that place, though there was a great deal of energetic organic life—long snaking brambles thrust between the stones for a place in the light, tombstones and angels alike wore bushy coats of gripping ivy, shining in the wind and the wet, as the leaves moved very slightly. Ines looked at the repeated stone people. Several had lost their hands, and lifted blind stumps to the grey air. These were less upsetting than those who were returning to formlessness, and had fists that seemed rotted by leprosy. Someone had come and sliced the heads from the necks of several cherubs—recently, the severed edges were still an even white. The stony representations of floating things—feathered wings, blossom and petals—made Ines feel queasy, for they were inert and weighed down, they were pulled towards the earth and what was under it.

Once or twice she saw things which spoke to her own condition. A glint of gold in the tesserae of a mosaic pavement over a house whose ascription was hopelessly obscured. A sarcophagus on pillars, lead-lined, human-sized, planted with spring bulbs, and, she thought, almost certainly ancient and pagan, for it was surrounded with a company of eyeless elders in Etruscan robes, standing each in his pillared alcove. Their faces were rubbed away, but their substance—some kind of rosy marble?—had erupted into facets and flakes that glinted in the gloom like her own surfaces.

She might take her place near them, she thought, but was dissuaded by the aspect of their neighbours, a group of the theological virtues, Faith, Hope and Charity, simpering lifeless women clutching a stone cross, a stone anchor, and a fat stone helpless child. They had nothing to do with a woman who was made up of volcanic glass and semi-precious stones, who needed a refuge for her end. No, that was not true. They were not nothing to do with her, for they frightened her. She did not want to stand, unmoving, amongst them. She began to imagine an indefinite half-life, looking like them, yet staring out of seeing eyes. She walked faster.

Round the edges of the vast field of stones, within the spiky confine of the wall, was a shrubbery, with narrow paths and a few stone benches and compost bins. As she went into the bushes, she heard a sound, the chink of hammer on stone. She stood still. She heard it again. Thinking to surprise a vandal, she rounded a corner, and came upon a rough group of huts and a stack of stony rubble.

One of the huts was a long open shelter, wooden-walled and tile-roofed. It contained a trestle table, behind which a man was working, with a stone-mason's hammer and chisel. He was a big muscular man, with a curly golden beard, a tanned skin, and huge hands. Behind him stood a gaggle of stone women, in various states of disrepair, lipless, fingerless, green-stained, soot-streaked. There was also a heap of urns, and the remains of one or two of the carved arti-ficial rocks on which various symbolic objects had once been planted. He made a gesture as if to cover up what he was doing, which appeared, from the milky sheen of the marble, to be new work, rather than restoration.

Ines sidled up. She had almost given up speech, for her voice scratched and whistled oddly in her petrify-ing larynx. She shopped with gestures, as though she was an Eastern woman, robed and veiled, too timid, or linguistically inept, to ask about things. The stone-cutter looked up at her, and down at his work, and made one or two intent little chips at it. Ines felt the sharp blows in her own body. He looked across at her. She whispered—whispering was still possible and normal—that she would like to see what he was mak-ing. He shrugged, and then stood aside, so that she could look. What she saw was a loose-limbed child lying on a large carved cushion, its arms flung out, its legs at unexpected angles, its hair draggled across its smooth forehead, its eyes closed in sleep. No, Ines saw, not sleep. This child was a dead child, its limbs were relaxed in death. Because it was dead, its form intimated painfully that it had once been alive. The whole had a blurred effect, because the final sharps and rounds had not been clarified. It had no navel; its little stomach was rough. Ines said what came into her stone head.

"No one will want that on any kind of monument. It's dead."

The stonecutter did not speak.

"They write on their stones," Ines said, "he fell asleep on such a day, she is sleeping. It's not sleep."

"I am making this for myself," he said. "I do repair work here, it is a living. But I do my own work also."

His voice was large and warm. He said:

"Are you looking for any person's grave here? Or perhaps visiting—"

Ines laughed. The sound was pebbly. She said, "No, I am thinking about my own final resting-place. I have problems."

He offered her a seat, which she refused, and a plastic cup of coffee from a thermos, which she accepted though she was not thirsty, to oil her voice and to make an excuse for lingering. She whispered that she would like to see more of his work, of his own work.

"I am interested in stone work," she said. "Maybe you can make me a monument."

As if in answer to this, he brought out from under his bench various wrapped objects, a heavy sphere, a pyramid, a bag of small rattling objects. He moved slowly and deliberately, laying out before her a stone angel-head, a sculpted cairn, a collection of hands and feet, large and small. All were originally the typical funereal carvings of the place. He had pierced and fretted and embellished them with forms of life that were alien and contradictory, yet part of them. Fingers and toes became prisms and serpents, minuscule faces peered between toes and tiny bodies of mice or marmosets gripped toenails or lay around wrists like Celtic dragons. The cairn—from a distance blockish like all the rest—was alive with marine creatures in whose bellies sat creatures, whose faces peered out of oyster-shells and from carved rib-cages, neither human faces nor inhuman. And the dead stone angel-face had been made into a round mass of superimposed face on face, in bas-relief and fretwork, faces which shared eyes and profiles, mouths which fed two divergent starers with four eyes and serpents for hair. He said:

"I am not supposed to appropriate things which belong here. But I take the lost ones, the detached ones without a fixed place, I look for the life in them."

"Pygmalion."

"Hardly. You like them?"

"Like is the wrong word. They are alive."

He laughed. "Stones are alive where I come from."

"Where?" she breathed.

"I am an Icelander. I work here in the winter, and go home in the summer, when the nights are bright.

I show my work—my own work—in Iceland in the summer."

She wondered dully where she would be when he was in Iceland in the summer. He said:

"If you like, I will give you something. A small thing, and if you like to live with it, I will perhaps make you that monument."

He held out to her a small, carved hand which contained a basilisk and two mussel shells. When she took it from him, it chinked, stone on stone, against her awkward fingertips. He heard the sound, and took hold of her knobby wrist through her garments.

"I must go now," she breathed.

"No, wait, wait," he said.

But she pulled away, and hurried in the dusk, towards the iron gate.

THAT EVENING, she understood she might have been wrong about her immediate fate. She put the stone hand on her desk and went into the kitchen to make herself bread and cheese. She was trembling with exertion and emotion, with fear of stony enclosure and complicated anxiety about the Icelander. The bread-knife slipped as she struggled to cut the soft loaf, and sliced into her stone hand, between finger and thumb. She felt pain, which surprised her, and the spurt of hot blood from the wound whose depth she could not gauge. She watched the thick red liquid run down the back of her hand, on to the bread, on to the table. It was ruddy-gold, running in long glassy strings, and where it touched the bread, the bread went up in smoke, and where it touched the table, it hissed and smoked and bored its hot way through the wood and dripped, a duller red now, on to the plastic floor, which it singed with amber circles and puckering. Her veins were full of molten lava. She put out the tiny fires and threw away the burned bread. She thought, I am not going to stand in the rain and grow moss. I may erupt. I do not know how that will be. She stood with the bread-knife in her hand and considered the rough stripes her blood had seared into the steel. She felt panic. To become stone is a figure, however fantastic, for death. But to become molten lava and to contain a furnace?

SHE WENT BACK the next day to the graveyard. Her clashing heart quickened when she heard the tap of hammer on stone, as she swung into the shrubbery. It was a pale blue wintry day, with pewter storm-clouds gathering. There was the Icelander, turning a glinting sphere in his hand, and squinting at it. He nodded amiably in her direction. She said:

"I want to show you something."

He looked up. She said:

"If anyone can bear to look, perhaps you can."

He nodded.

She began to undo her fastenings, pulling down zips, unhooking the hood under her chin, shaking free her musical crystalline hair, shrugging her monumental arms out of their bulky sleeves. He stared intently. She stripped off shirt and jogging pants, trainers and vest, her mother's silken knickers. She stood in front of him in her roughly gleaming patchwork, a human form vanishing under outcrops of silica, its lineaments suggested by veins of blue john that vanished into crusts of pumice and agate. She looked out of her cavernous eye sockets through salty eyes at the man, whose blue eyes considered her grotesque transformation. He looked. She croaked, "Have you ever seen such a thing?"

"Never," he said. "Never."

Hot liquid rose to the sills of her eyes and clattered in pearly drops on her ruddy haematite cheeks.

He stared. She thought, he is a man, and he sees me as I am, a monster.

"Beautiful," he said. "Grown, not crafted."

"You said that the stones in your country were alive. I thought you might understand what has happened to me. I do not need a monument. I have grown into one."

"I have heard of such things. Iceland is a country where we are matter-of-fact about strange things. We know we live in a world of invisible beings that exists in and around our own. We make gates in rocks for elves to come and go. But as well as living things without solid substance we know that rocks and stones have their own energies. Iceland is a young country, a restless country—in our land the earth's mantle is shaped at great speed by the churning of geysers and the eruption of lava and the progress of glaciers. We live like lichens, clinging to standing stones and rolling stones and heaving stones and rattling stones and flying stones. Our tales are full of striding stone women. We have mostly not given up the expectation of seeing them. But I did not expect to meet one here, in this dead place."

She told him how she had supposed that to be petrified was to be motionless. I was looking for a place to rest, she told him. She told him about the spurt of lava from her hand and showed him the black scar, fringed with a rime of new crystals.

"I think now, Iceland is where I should go, to find somewhere to—stand, or stay."

"Wait for the spring," he said, "and I will take you there. We have endless nights in the winter, and snowstorms, and the roads are impassable. In summer we have—briefly—endless days. I spend my winters here and my summers in my own country, climbing and walking."

"Maybe it will be over—maybe I shall be— finished—before the spring."

"I do not think so. But we will watch over it. Turn around, and let me see your back. It is beautiful beyond belief, and its elements are not constant."

"I have the sense that—the crust—is constantly thickening."

"There is an idea—for a sculptor—in every inch of it," he said.

HE SAID that his name was Thorsteinn Hallmundursson. He could not keep his eyes off her though his manner was always considered and gentle. Over the winter and into the early spring, they constructed a friendship. Ines allowed Thorsteinn to study her ridges and clefts. He touched her lightly, with padded fingers, and electricity flickered in her veining. He showed her samples of new stones as they sprouted in and on her body. The two she loved most were labradorite and fantomqvartz. Labradorite is dark blue, soft black, full of gleaming lights, peacock and gold and silver, like the aurora borealis embedded in hardness. In fantomqvartz, a shadowy crystal contains other shadowy crystals growing at angles in its transparent depths. Thorsteinn chipped and polished to bring out the lights and the angles, and in the end, as she came to trust him completely, Ines came to take pleasure in allowing him to decorate her gnarled fingers, to smooth the plane of her shin, and to reveal the hidden lights under the polished skin of her breasts. She discovered a new taste for sushi, for the iodine in seaweed and the salt taste of raw fish, so she brought small packs of these things to the shelter, and Thorsteinn gave her sips of peaty Laphroaig whisky from a hipflask he kept in his capacious fleecy coat. She did not come to love the graveyard, but familiarity made her see it differently.

It was a city graveyard, on which two centuries of soot had fallen. Although inner cities are now sanctuaries for wild things poisoned and starved in the countryside, the forms of life among the stones, though plump, lacked variety. Every day the fat pigeons gathered on the roof of Thorsteinn's shelter, catching the pale sunlight on their burnished feathers, mole-grey, dove-grey, sealskin-grey. Every day the fat squirrels lolloped busily from bush to bush, their grey tails and faces tinged with ginger, their strong little claws gripping. There were magpies, and strutting crows. There was thick bright moss moving swiftly (for moss) over the stones and their carved names. Thorsteinn said he did not like to clean it away, it was beautiful. Ines said she had noticed there were few lichens, and Thorsteinn said that lichens only grew in clean air; pollution destroyed them easily. In Iceland he would show her mosses and lichens she could never have dreamed of. He told her tales, through the city winter, as the cold rain dripped, and the cemetery crust froze, and cracked, and melted into mud-puddles, of a treeless landscape peopled by inhuman beings, laughing weightless elves, hidden heavy-footed, heavy-handed trolls. Ines's own crust grew thicker and more rugged. She had to learn to speak all over again, a mixture of whistles and clicks and solo gestures which perhaps only the Icelander would have understood.

WINTER BECAME SPRING, the dead leaves became dark with rain, grass pushed through them, crocuses and snowdrops, followed by self-spread bluebells and an uncontrollable carpet of celandine, pale gold flowers with flat green leaves, which ran over everything, headstones and gravel, bottle-green marble chips on recently dug graves, Thorsteinn's heap of rubble. They lasted a brief time, and then the gold faded to silver, and the silver became white, transparent, a brief ghostly lace of fine veins, and then a fallen mulch of mould, inhabited by pushy tendrils and the creamy nodes of rhizomes.

The death of the celandines seemed to be the signal for departure. They had discussed how this should be done. Ines had assumed they would fly to Reykjavík, but when she came to contemplate such a journey, she saw that it was impossible. Not only could she not fold her new body into the small space of a canvas bucket seat that would likely not bear her weight. She could never pass through the security checks at the airport. How would a machine react to the ores and nuggets scattered in her depths? If she were asked to pull back her hood, the airport staff would run screaming. Or shoot her. She did not know if she could now be killed by a bullet.

Thorsteinn said they could go by sea. From Scotland to Bergen in Norway, from Bergen to Seydhisfjördhur in East Iceland. They would be seven days on the ocean.

THEY BOOKED A PASSAGE on a small trading boat that had four cabins for passengers, and a taciturn crew. They put in at the Faroe Islands and then went out into the Atlantic, between towering rock-faces, with no shore, no foam breaking at the base. In the swell of the Atlantic the ship nosed its way between great green and white walls of travelling water, in a fine salt spray. The sky changed and changed, opal and gun-metal, grass-green and crimson, mussel-blue and velvet black, scattered with wild starshine. Thorsteinn and Ines stood on deck whenever they could, and looked out ahead of them. Ines did not look back. She tasted the salt on her black-veined tongue, and thought of the biblical woman who had become a pillar of salt when she looked back. She was no pillar. She was heaving and restless like the sea. When she thought of her past life, it was vague in her new mind, like cobwebs. Her mother was now to her flying dust in air, motes of bonemeal settling on the foam-flowers in the beck where she had scattered her. She could barely remember their peaceful meals together, the dry wit of her mother's observations, the glow of the flames in the ceramic coal in the gas fire in the hearth. She opened her tent of garments to the driving wind and wet. She had found her feet easily and did not feel seasick. Thorsteinn rode the deck beside her like a lion or a war-horse, smiling through his beard.

She was interested in his human flesh. She found in herself a sprouting desire to take a bite out of him, his cheek or his neck, out of a mixture of some sort of affection and curiosity to see what the sensation would be like. She resisted the impulse easily enough, though she licked her teeth—razor-sharp flinty incisors, grim granite molars. She thought human thoughts and stone thoughts. The latter were slow, patchily coloured, textured and extreme, both hot and cold. They did not translate into the English language, or into any other she knew: they were things that accumulated, solidly, knocked against each other, heaped and slipped.

Thorsteinn, like all Icelanders, became more animated as they neared his island. He told tales of early settlers, including St. Brendan, who had sailed there in the fifth century, riding the seas in a hide coracle, and had been beaten back by a huge hairy being, armed with a pair of tongs and a burning mass of incandescent slag, which he hurled at the retreating monks. St. Brendan believed he had come to Ultima Thule; the volcano, Mt. Hekla, was the entrance to Hell at the edge of the world. The Vikings came in the ninth century. Thorsteinn, standing on deck at night with Ines, was amazed to discover that the back of her hands was made of cordierite, grey-blue crystals mixed with a sandy colour, rough and undistinguished but which, held at a certain angle, revealed facets like shimmering dragon-scales. The Vikings, he told her, had used the way this mineral polarised light to navigate in the dark, using the Polar Star and the moonlight. He made her turn her heavy hands, flashing and winking in the darkness, as the water-drops flashed on ropes and crest-curls of wake.

Her first vision of Iceland was of the wild jagged peaks of the eastern fjords. Thorsteinn packed them into a high rugged truck-like car, and they drove south, along the wild coast, past ancient volcanic valleys, sculpted, slowly, slowly, by Ice Age glaciers. They were under the influence, literally—of the great glacier, Vatnajökull, the largest in Europe, Thorsteinn said, sitting easily at the wheel. Brown thick rivers rushed down crevices and into valleys, carrying alluvial dust. They glimpsed the sheen of it from mountain passes, and then, as they came to the flatlands of the south, they saw the first glacial tongues pouring down into the plains, white and shining above the green marshes and under the blue sky. Thorsteinn alternated between a steady silence and a kind of incantatory recitation of history, geography, time before history, myth. His country appeared to her old, when she first saw it, a primal chaos of ice, stone silt, black sand, gold mud. His stories went easily back to the first and second centuries, or the Middle Ages, as though they were yesterday, and his own ancestors figured in tales of enmity and banishment as though they were uncles and kinsmen who had sat down to eat with him last year. And yet, the striking thing, the decisive thing, about this landscape, was that it was geologically young. It was turbulent with the youth and energy of an unsettled crust of the earth. The whole south coast of Iceland is still being changed—in a decade, in a twinkling of an eye—by volcanic eruptions which pour red-hot magma from mountain ridges, or spout up, boiling, from under the thick-ribbed ice. This is a recent lava field, said Thorsteinn, as they came to the Skaftáhraun, this was made by the eruption of the Lakagígar in 1783, which lasted for a year, and killed over half the population and over half the livestock. Ines stared impassively at the fine black sand-drifts, and felt the red-hot liquid boil a little, in her belly, in her lungs.

They travelled on, over the great black plain of Myrdalssandur. This, said Thorsteinn, was the work of a volcano, Katla, which erupted under a glacier, Myrdalsjökull. There is a troll-woman connected to this volcano, he told her. She was called Katla, which is a feminine version of ketill, kettle, and she was said to have hidden a kettle of molten gold, which could be seen by human eyes on one day of the year only. But those who set out to find it were troubled by false visions and strange sights—burning homesteads, slaughtered livestock—and turned back from the quest in panic. Katla was the owner of a pair of magic breeches, which made her a very fleet runner, leaping lightly from crag to crag, descending the mountain-scree like smoke. They were said to be made from human skin. A young shepherd took them once, to help him catch his sheep, and Katla caught him, killed him, dismembered him, and hid his body in a barrel of whey. They found him, of course, when the whey was drunk, and Katla fled, running like clouds in the wind, over to Myrdalsjökull, and was never seen again.

Was she a stone woman? asked Ines. Her stony thoughts rumbled around heavy limbs made supple by borrowed skin. Her own human skin was flaking away, like the skins snakes and lizards rub off against stones and branches, revealing the bright sleekness beneath. She picked it away with crystal fingertips, scratching the dead stuff out of the crevices of elbow, knee-joint and her non-existent navel.

Thorsteinn said there was no mention of her being stone. There were trolls in Iceland who turned to stone, like Norse trolls, if the sun hit them. But by no means all were of that kind. There were trolls, he said, who slept for centuries amongst the stones of the desert, or along the riverbeds, and stirred with an earthquake, or an eruption, into new life. There were human trolls, distinguishable only by their huge size from farmers and fishermen. "Personally," said Thorsteinn, "I do not think you are a troll. I think you are a metamorphosis."

THEY CAME TO REYKJAVÍK, the smoky harbour. Ines was uneasy, even in this small city—she strode, hooded and bundled behind Thorsteinn, as he showed her the harbour. Something was to happen, and it was not here, not amongst humans. New thoughts growled between her marbled ears: Thorsteinn wandered in and out of chandlers' and artists' stores, and his uncouth protégée stood in the shadows and more or less hissed between her teeth. She asked where they were going, and he said—as though she should have read his thoughts—that they were going to his summer house, where he would work.

"And I?" she said, grumbling. Thorsteinn stared at her, assessing and unsmiling.

"I don't know," he said. "Neither of us can know. I am taking you where there are known to be creatures—not human. That may be a good or a bad thing, I am a sculptor not a seer, how can I know? What I do hope is that you will allow me to record you. To make works that show what you are. For I may never see such a thing again."

She smiled, showing all her teeth in the shadow of her hood.

"I agree," she said.

THEY DROVE WEST AGAIN, from Reykjavík, along the ring road. They saw wonders—steam pouring from mountain-sides, hot blue water bubbling in stony pots in the earth, the light sooty pumice, the shrouded humped black form of Hekla, hooded and violent.

Thorsteinn remarked casually that it had erupted in 1991 and was still unusually active, under the earth and under the ice. They were heading for the valley of Thorsmork, Thor's Forest, which lay inaccessibly between three glaciers, two deep rivers, and a string of dark mountains. They crossed torrents, and ground along the dirt road. There were no other humans, but the fields were full of wild flowers, and birds sang in birches and willows. Now it is summer, said Thorsteinn. In the winter you cannot come here. The rivers are impassable. You cannot stand against the wind.

Thorsteinn's summer house was not unlike his encampment in the graveyard, although it was likely that the influence was the other way. It was built into a hillside, walled and roofed with turf, with a rough outbuilding, also turf-roofed, with his long work-table. It was roughly furnished: there were two heavy wooden bedsteads, a stone sink through which springwater ran from a channelled pipe in the hillside, a table, chairs, a wooden cupboard. And a hearth, with a stove. They had a view—when the weather was clear—across a wide valley, and a turbulent glacial river, to the sharp dark ridges of the mountains and the distant bright sheen of the glacier. The grassy space in front of the house looked something between a chaos of boulders and a half-formed stone circle. Ines came to see that all the stones, from the vast and cow-sized to clusters of pebbles and polished singletons, were works in progress, or potential works, or works finished for the time being. They were both carved and decorated. A discovered face peered from under a crusty overhang, one-eyed, fanged, leering. A boulder displayed a perfectly polished pair of youthful breasts, glistening in circles of golden lichen. Cracks made by ice, channels worn by water, mazes where roots had pushed and twisted, were coloured in brilliant pinks and golds, glistening where the light caught them. Nests of stony eggs made of sooty pumice, or smooth thulite, were inhabited by crystal worms and serpentine adders.

The stonecarver worked with the earth and the weather as his assistants or controllers. A hunched stone woman had a fantastic garden of brilliant moss spilling from her lap and over her thighs. An upright monolith was fantastically adorned with the lirellate fruiting bodies of the "writing lichens." On closer inspection, Ines saw that jewels had been placed in crevices, and sharpened pins like medieval cloak-brooches had been inserted in holes threaded in the stone surface. A dwarfish stone had tiny, carved gold hands where its ears might have been expected to be.

Thorsteinn said that he liked—in the summer—to add to the durable stones work that mimicked and reflected the fantastic succession of the weathers of that land. He suspended ingenious structures of plastic string, bubble-wrap, polyurethane sheeting, to make ice, rain-floods, the bubbling of geysers and mud-baths. He made rainbows of strips of glass, and bent them above his creatures, catching the bright blue light in the steely storm-light and the wet shimmer of enveloping cloud in their reflections.

There were many real rainbows. There could be several climates in a day—bright sun, gathering storm, snowfall, great coils and blasts of wind so violent that a man could not stand up—though the stone woman found herself taking pleasure in standing against the turbulent air as a surfer rides a wave, when even Thorsteinn had had to take shelter. There were flowers in the early brief summer—saxifrages and stonecrops, lady's bedstraw and a profusion of golden angelica. They walked out into soft grey carpets of *Cetraria islandica,* the lichen that is known as "Iceland moss." Reindeer food, human food, possible cancer cure, said Thorsteinn.

He asked her, rather formally, over a fireside supper of smoked lamb and scrambled eggs, whether she would sit for him. It was light in the northern night: his face was fiery in the midnight sun, his beard was full of gold, and brass, and flame-flickering. She had not looked at herself since they left England. She did not carry a mirror, and Thorsteinn's walls were innocent of reflecting surfaces, though there were sacks of glass mosaic tesserae in the workshop. She said she did not know if she any longer differed from the stones he collected and decorated so tactfully, so spectacularly. Maybe he should not make her portrait, but decorate her, carve into her, when . . . When whatever was happening had come to its end, she left unsaid, for she could not imagine its end. She tore at the tasty lamb with her sharp teeth. She had an overwhelming need for meat, which she did not acknowledge. She ground the fibres in the mill of her jaws. She said, she would be happy to do what she could.

Thorsteinn said that she *was,* what he had only imagined. All my life I have made things about metamorphosis. *Slow* metamorphoses, in human terms. Fast, fast in terms of the earth we inhabit. You are a walking metamorphosis. Such as a man meets only in dreams. He raised his wineglass to her. I too, he said, am utterly changed by your changing. I want to make a record of it. She said she would be honoured, and meant it.

TIME TOO WAS PARADOXICAL in Iceland. The summer was a fleeting island of light and brightness in a shroud of thick vapours and freezing needles of ice in the air. But within the island of the summer the daylight was sempiternal, there was no nightfall, only the endless shifts in the colour of the sky, trout-dappled, mackerel-shot, turquoise, sapphire, peridot, hot transparent red, and, as the autumn put out boisterous fingers, flowing with the gyrating and swooping veils of the aurora borealis. Thorsteinn worked all summer to his own rhythm, which was stubborn and earthy—long, long hours—and rapid, like waterfalls, or air currents. Ines sat on a stone bench, and occasionally did domestic things with inept stony fingers, hulled a few peas, scrubbed a potato, whisked a bowl of eggs. She tried reading, but her new eyes could not quite bring the dancing black letters to have any more meaning than the spiders and ants which scurried round her feet or mounted her stolid ankles. She preferred standing, really. Bending was harder and harder. So she stood, and stared at the hillside and the distant neb of the glacier. Some days they talked as he worked. Sometimes, for a couple of days together, they said nothing.

He made many, many drawings of her face, of her fingers, of her whole cragged form. He made small images in clay, and larger ones, cobbled together from stones and glass fragments and threads of things representing the weather, which the weather then disturbed. He made wreaths of wild flowers, which dried in the air, and were taken by the wind. He came close, and peered dispassionately into the crystal blocks of her eyes, which reflected the red light of the midnight sun. She made an increasing number of solitary forays into the landscape. When she returned, once, she saw from a great distance a standing stone that he had made, and saw that through its fantastic crust, under its tattered mantle, it was possible to see the lineaments of a beautiful woman, a woman with a carved, attentive face, looking up and out. The human likeness vanished as she came closer. She thought he had *seen* her, and this made her happy. He saw that she existed, in there.

But she found it harder and harder to see him. He began to seem blurred and out of focus, not only when his human blue eye peered into her crystal one and his beard fanned in a golden cloud round the disc of his face. He was becoming insubstantial. His very solid body looked as though it was simply a form of water vapour. She had to cup her basalt palm around her ear to hear his great voice, which sounded like the whispering of grasshoppers. She heard him snore at night, in the wooden bed, and the sound was indistinguishable from the gurgle of the water, or the prying random gusts of the wind.

And at the same time she was seeing, or almost seeing, things which seemed to crowd and gesture just beyond the range of her vision, behind her head, beyond the peripheral circle of her gaze. From the deck of the ship she had seen momentary sea creatures. Dolphins had rushed glistening amongst the long needles of air caught in the rush of their wake. Whales had briefly humped parts of guessed-at bulks through the wrinkling of the surface, the muscular span of a forked tail, the blast of a spout in a contracting air-hole in an unimaginable skin. Fulmars had appeared from nowhere in the flat sky and had plummeted like falling swords through the surface which closed over them. So now she sensed earth bubbles and earth monsters shrugging themselves into shape in the air and in the falling fosses. Fleet herds of light-footed creatures flowed round the house with the wind, and she almost saw, she sensed with some new sense, that they waved elongated arms in a kind of elastic mockery or ecstasy. Stones she stared at, as Thorsteinn worked on her images, began to dimple and shift, like disguised moor-birds, speckled and splotched, on nests of disguised eggs, speckled and splotched, in a wilderness of stones, speckled and splotched. Lichens seemed to grow at visible speeds and form rings and coils, with triangular heads like adders. Clearest of all—almost visible—were the huge dancers, forms that humped themselves out of earth and boulders, stamped and hurtled, beckoned with strong arms and snapping fingers. After long looking she seemed also to see that these things, the fleet and the portentous, the lithe and the stolid, were walking and running like parasites on the back of some moving beast so huge that the mountain range was only a wrinkle in its vasty hide, as it stirred in its slumber, or shook itself slightly as it woke.

She said to Thorsteinn in one of their economical exchanges:

"There are living things here I can almost see, but not see."

"Maybe, when you can see them," he said equably, scribbling away with charcoal, "maybe then . . ."

"I am very tired, most of the time. And when I am not, I am full of—quite *abnormal*—energy."

"That's good?"

"It's alarming."

"We shall see."

"Do humans in Iceland," she asked again, conscious that *something* was staring and listening—uncomprehending, she believed—to the scratch of her voice—"do humans turn into trolls?"

"Trolls," said Thorsteinn. "That's a human word for them. We have a word, *tryllast,* which means to go mad, to go berserk. Like trolls. Always from a human perspective. Which is a bit of a precarious perspective, here, in this land."

There was a long silence. Ines looked at his face as he worked, and could not focus the eyes that studied her so intently: they were charcoal blurs, full of dust-motes. Whereas the hillside was alive with eyes, that opened lazily within fringing mossy lashes, that stared through and past her from hollows in stones, that flashed in the light briefly and vanished again.

Thorsteinn said:

"There is a tale we tell of a group of poor men who went out to gather lichens for the winter. And one of them climbed higher than the others and the crag above him suddenly put out long stony arms, and wound them round him, and lifted him, and carried him up the hillside. The story says the stone was an old troll woman. His companions were very frightened and ran home. The next year, they went there again, and he came to meet them, over the moss carpet, and he was grey like the lichens. They asked him, was he happy, and he didn't answer. They asked him what he believed in, was he a Christian, and he answered dubiously that he believed in God and Jesus. He would not come with them and we get the impression that they did not try very hard to persuade him. The next year he was greyer and stood stock-still staring. When they asked him about his beliefs, he moved his mouth in his face, but no words came. And the next year, he came again, and they asked again what he believed in, and he replied, laughing fiercely, *Trunt, trunt, og tröllin í fjöllunum.*"

The English scholar who persisted in her said, "What does it mean?"

" '*Trunt, trunt*' is just nonsense, it means rubbish and junk and aha and hubble bubble, that sort of thing, I don't know an English expression that will do as a translation. Trunt trunt, and the trolls in the fells."

"It has a good rhythm."

"Indeed it does."

"I am afraid, Thorsteinn."

He put his bear-arm round the knobs and flinty edges that were where her shoulders had been. It felt to her lighter than cobweb.

"They call me," she said in a whisper. "Do you hear them?"

"No. But I know they call."

"They dance. At first it looked ugly, their rushing and stamping. But now—now I am also afraid that I can't—join the circle. I have never danced. And there is such wild energy." She tried to be precise. "I don't exactly *see* them still. But I do see their dancing, the furious form of it."

Thorsteinn said, "You will see them, when the time comes. I do believe you will."

As the autumn drew in she grew restless. She had planted small gardens in the crevices of her body, trailing grasses, liverworts. Creatures ran over her—insects first, a stone-coloured butterfly, indistinguishable from her speckled breast, foraging ants, a millipede. There were even fine red worms, the colour of raw meat, which burrowed unhindered. She began to walk more, taking these things with her. In September, they had several days of driving rain, frost was thick on the turf roof, the glacial rivers swelled and boiled and ice came down them in clumps and blocks, and also formed where the spray lay on the vegetation. Thorsteinn said that in a very little time it would be unsafe to stay— they might be cut off. He watched her brows contract over the glittering eyes in their hollow caves.

"I can't go back with you."

"You can. You are welcome to come with me."

"You know I must stay. You have always known. I am simply gathering up courage."

WHEN THE DAY CAME, it brought one of those Icelandic winds that howl across the earth, carrying away all unsecured objects and creatures, including men if they have no pole to clutch, no shelter built into the rock. Birds can make no way in such weather, they are blown back and broken. Snow and ice and hurtling cloud are in and on the wind, mixed with moving earth and water, and odd wreaths of steam gathered from geysers. Thorsteinn went into his house and held on to the doorpost. Ines began to come with him, and then turned away, looking up the mountainside, standing easily in the furious breakers of the moving air. She lifted a monumental arm and gestured towards the fells and then to her eyes. No one could be heard in this wailing racket, but he saw that she was signalling that now she saw them clearly. He nodded his head—he needed his arms to hang on to the doorpost. He looked up the mountain and saw, no doubt what she now saw clearly, figures, spinning and bowing in a rapid dance on huge, lithe, stony legs, beckoning with expansive gestures, flinging their great arms wide in invitation. The woman in his stone-garden took a breath—he saw her sides quiver—and essayed a few awkward dance-steps, a sweep of an arm, of both arms. He heard her laughter in the wind. She jigged a little, as though gathering momentum, and then began a dancing run, into the blizzard. He heard a stone voice, shouting and singing, *"Trunt, trunt, og tröllin í fjöllunum."*

He went in, and closed his door against the weather, and began to pack.

Raw Material

HE ALWAYS TOLD THEM the same thing, to begin with "Try to avoid falseness and strain. Write what you really know about. Make it new. Don't invent melodrama for the sake of it. Don't try to run, let alone fly, before you can walk with ease." Every year, he glared amiably at them. Every year they wrote melodrama. They clearly needed to write melodrama. He had given up telling them that Creative Writing was not a form of psychotherapy. In ways both sublime and ridiculous it clearly was, precisely, that.

The class had been going for fifteen years. It had moved from a schoolroom to a disused Victorian church, made over as an Arts and Leisure Centre. The village was called Sufferacre, which was thought to be a corruption of *sulfuris aquae.* It was a failed Derbyshire spa. It was his home town. In the 1960s he had written a successfully angry, iconoclastic and shocking novel called *Bad Boy.* He had left for London and fame, and returned quietly, ten years later. He lived in a caravan in somebody's paddock. He travelled widely, on a motor bike, teaching Creative Writing in pubs, schoolrooms and arts centres. His name was Jack Smollett. He was a big, shuffling, smiling, red-faced man, with longish blond hair, who wore cable-knit sweaters in oily colours, and bright scarlet necker-chiefs. Women liked him, as they liked enthusiastic Labrador dogs. They felt, almost all—and his classes were predominantly female—more desire to cook apple pies and Cornish pasties for him, than to make violent love to him. They believed he didn't eat sensi-bly. (They were right.) Now and then, someone in one of his classes would point out, as he exhorted them to stick to what they knew, that they themselves were what he "really knew." Will you write about *us,* Jack? No, he always said, that would be a betrayal of con-fidence. You should always respect other people's privacy. Creative writing teachers had something in common with doctors, even if—yet again—creative writing wasn't therapy.

In fact, he had tried unsuccessfully to sell two dif-ferent stories based on the confessions (or inventions) of his class. They offered themselves to him like raw oysters on pristine plates. They told him horror and bathos, day-dreams, vituperation and vengeance. They couldn't write, their inventions were crude, and he couldn't find a way to perform the necessary opera-tions to spin the muddy straw into silk, or turn the raw bleeding chunks into a savoury dish. So he kept faith with them, not entirely voluntarily. He did care about writing. He cared about writing more than any-thing, sex, food, beer, fresh air, even warmth. He wrote and rewrote perpetually, in his caravan. He was rewriting his fifth novel. *Bad Boy,* his first, had been written in a rush just out of the sixth form, and snapped up by the first publisher he'd sent it to. It was what he had expected. (Well, it was one of two scenarios that played in his young brain, immediate recognition, painful, dedicated struggle. When success happened it appeared blindingly clear that it had always been the only possible outcome.) So he didn't go to university, or learn a trade. He was, as he knew he was, a Writer. His second novel, *Smile and Smile,* had sold 600 copies, and was remaindered. His third and his fourth—frequently rewritten—lay in brown paper, stamped and restamped, in a tin chest in the caravan. He didn't have an agent.

CLASSES RAN from September to March. In the sum-mer he worked in literary festivals, or holiday camps on sunny islands. He was pleased to see the classes again in September. He still thought of himself as wild and unattached, but he was a creature of habit. He liked things to happen at precise, recurring times, in precise, recurring ways. More than half of most of his classes were old faithfuls who came back year after year. Each class had a nucleus of about ten. At the beginning of the year this was often doubled by enthusiastic newcomers. By Christmas many of these would have dropped away, seduced by other courses, or intimidated by the regulars, or overcome by domestic drama or personal lassitude. St. Antony's Leisure Centre was gloomy because of its high roof, and draughty because of its ancient doors and windows. The class themselves had brought oil heaters, and a circle of standard lamps with imitation stained-glass covers. The old churchy chairs were pushed into a circle, under these pleasant lights.

HE LIKED THE LISTS of their names. He liked words, he was a writer. Sometimes he talked about how much Nabokov had got out of the list of names of Lolita's class-mates, how much of America, how strong an image from how few words. Sometimes he tried to make an imaginary list that would please him as much as the real one. It never worked. He would write allusive equivalents—Vicar, say, for Parson, Gold, for Silver, and find his text inexorably resubstituting the precise concatenation that existed. His current class ran:

> Abbs, Adam
> Archer, Megan
> Armytage, Blossom
> Forster, Bobby
> Fox, Cicely

Hogg, Martin
Parson, Anita
Pearson, Amanda
Pygge, Gilly
Secrett, Lola
Secrett, Tamsin
Silver, Annabel
Wheelwright, Rosy

He consulted this for pointless symmetries. Pygge and Hogg. Pearson and Parson. The prevalence of As and absence of Es and Rs. He had kept a register, for a time, of surnames reflecting ancient, vanished occupations—Archer, Forster, Parson, Wheelwright. Were there more in Derbyshire than in other places?

Then there was the list of the occupations, also a flawed microcosm.

Abbs	deacon in the C. of E.
Archer	estate agent
Armytage	vet
Forster	redundant bank teller
Fox	eighty-two-year-old spinster
Hogg	accountant
Parson	schoolmistress
Pearson	farmer
Pygge	nurse
Secrett, Lola	intermittent student, daughter of

Secrett, Tamsin	living on alimony (her own phrase)
Silver	librarian
Wheelwright	student (engineering)

The most recent work they had produced was:

Adam Abbs	A tale of the martyrdom of nuns in Rwanda
Megan Archer	A story of the prolonged rape and abduction of an estate agent
Blossom Armytage	A tale of the elaborate torture of two Sealyham dogs
Bobby Forster	A tale of the entrapment and vengeful slaughter of an unjust driving examiner
Cicely Fox	How we used to black-lead stoves
Martin Hogg	Hanging, drawing and quartering under Henry VIII
Anita Parson	A tale of unreported, persistent child abuse and Satanic sacrifice
Amanda Pearson	A tale of a cheating husband hacked down by his vengeful wife with an axe
Gilly Pygge	Clever murder by a cruel surgeon during an operation

Lola Secrett	The nervous breakdown of a menopausal woman with a beautiful and patient daughter
Tamsin Secrett	The nervous breakdown of a feckless teenager with a wise but powerless mother
Annabel Silver	A sado-masochistic initiation of a girl sold into white slavery in North Africa
Rosy Wheelwright	A cycle of very explicit lesbian love poems involving motor bikes.

He had learned the hard way not to involve himself in any way in their lives. When he first moved into the caravan he had had a conventional enough vision of its warm confinement as a secret place to take women, for romping, for intimacy, for summer nights of naked-ness and red wine. He had scanned his new classes, fairly obviously, for hopefuls, measuring breasts, admiring ankles, weighing pink round mouths against wide red ones against unpainted severe ones. He had had one or two really good athletic encounters, one or two tearful failures, one overkill which had left him with a staring, shivering watcher every night at the gate of his paddock, or occasionally peering wildly through the caravan window.

Creative writers are creative writers. Descriptions of his bedlinen, his stove, the blasts of wind on his caravan walls, began to appear, ever more elaborated, in the stories that were produced for general criticism. Competitive descriptions of his naked body began to be circulated. Heartless or cowering males (depending on the creative writer) had thickets, or wiry fuzzes, or fur soft as a dog fox, or scratchy-bristly reddish outcrops of hair on their chests. One or two descriptions of fierce thrusting and pubic clamping were followed by anticlimax, both in life and in art. He gave up—ever—taking women from his classes on to his unfolded settee. He gave up, ever, talking to his students one at a time or differentiating between them. The sex-in-a-caravan theme wilted and did not resuscitate. His stalker went to a pottery class, transferred her affections, and made stubby pottery pillars, glazed with flames and white spray. As the folklore of his sex life diminished he became mysterious and authoritative and found he enjoyed it. The barmaid of the Wig and Quill came round on Sundays. He couldn't find the right words to describe her orgasms—prolonged events with staccato and shivering rhythms alternating oddly—and this teased and pleased him.

He sat alone in the bar of the Wig and Quill the evening before his class, reading the "stories" that were to be returned. Martin Hogg had discovered the torture which consists of winding out the living intestines on a spindle. He couldn't write, which Jack thought was just as well—he used words like "gruesome" and "horrible" a lot, but was unable, perhaps inevitably, to raise in a reader's mind any image of an intestine, a spindle, pain, or an executioner. Jack supposed that Martin was enjoying himself, but even that was not very well conveyed to his putative reader. Jack was more impressed by Bobby Forster's fantasy of the slaughter of a driving examiner. This had some plot to it—involving handcuffs, severed brake cables, the removal of signs indicating quicksands, even an unbreakable alibi for the mild man who had turned on his tormentor. Forster occasionally produced a sharp, etched sentence that was memorable. Jack had found one of these in Patricia Highsmith, and another, by sheer chance, in Wilkie Collins. He had dealt with this plagiarism, rather neatly, he thought, by underlining the sentences and writing in the margin "I have always said that reading excellent writers, and absorbing them, is essential to good writing. But it should not go quite so far as plagiarism." Forster was a white-faced, precise person, behind round glasses. (His hero was neat and pale, with glasses which made it hard to see what he was thinking.) He said mildly, on both occasions, that the plagiarism was unconscious, must have been a trick of memory. Unfortunately this led Jack to suspect automatically that any other excrescent elegance was also a plagiarism.

HE CAME to "How We Used to Black-lead Stoves." Cicely Fox was a new student. Her contribution was hand-written—with pen and ink, not even felt-tip. She had given the work to him with a deprecating note.

"I don't know if this is the sort of thing you meant when you said 'Write what you really know about.' I was sorry to find that there were so many *lacunae* in my memory. I do hope you will forgive them. The writing may not be of interest, but the exercise was pleasurable."

How We Used to Black-lead Stoves

It is strange to think of activities that were once so much part of our lives that they seemed daily inevitable, like waking and sleeping. At my age, these things come back in their contingent quiddity, things we did with quick fingers and backs that bent without precaution. It is today's difficult slitting of plastic wraps, or brilliantly blinking microwave LED displays, that seem like veils and shadows.

Take black-leading. The kitchen-ranges in the kitchens of our childhood and young lives were great, darkly gleaming chests of fierce heat. Their frontage was covered with heavy hasped doors, opening on various ovens, large and small, various flues, the furnace itself, where the fuel went in. Words are needed for extremes of blackness and brightness. Brightness included the gold-glitter of the rail along the front of the range, where the tea-towels hung, and the brass knobs on certain of the little doors which had to be burnished with Brasso—a sickly yellowish powdery liquid—every morning. It included also the roaring flame within and under the heavy cast-iron box. If you opened the door, when it was fully burning, you could hear and see it—a flickering transparent sheet of scarlet and yellow, shot with blue, shot with white, flashing purple, roaring and burping and piffing. You could immediately see it dying in the rusty edges of the embers. It was important to close the door quickly, to keep the fire "in." "In" meant *contained,* and also meant, alight.

There were so many different blacks around that range. Various fuels were burned in it, unlike modern Agas which take oil, or anthracite. I remember coal. Coal has its own brightness, a gloss, a sheen. You can see the compacted layers of dead wood—millions of years dead—in the strata on the faces of the chunks of good coal. They shine. They give out a black sparkle. The trees ate the sun's energy and the furnace will release it. Coal is glossy. Coke is matt, and looks (indeed is) twice-burned, like volcano lava; the dust on coal glitters like glass dust, the dust on coke absorbs light, is soft, is inert. Some of it comes in little regular pressed cushions, like pillows for dead dolls, I used to think, or twisted humbugs for small demons. We ourselves were fed on charcoal for stomach upsets which may explain why I considered the edibility of these lumps. Or maybe even as a small child, I saw the open mouth of the furnace as a hell-hole. You were drawn in. You wanted to get closer and closer; you wanted to be able to turn away. And we were taught at school, about our own internal combustion of matter. The ovens behind other doors of the range, might conceal the puffed, risen shapes of loaves and teacakes, with that best of all smells, baking yeast dough, or the only slightly less delightful smell of the crust of a hot cake, toasted sugar, milk and egg. Now and then—the old ranges were temperamental—a batch of buns in frilled paper cups would come out black and smoking and stinking of destruction, ghastly analogies of the cinder-cushions. From there, I thought, came the cinders that fell from the mouths of bad children in fairy-tales, or stuffed their Christmas stockings.

The whole range was bathed in an aura of kept-down soot. In front of our own, at one time, was a peg-rug made by my father, by hooking strips of colourful scraps of cloth—old flannel shirts, old trousers—through sacking, and knotting them. Soot infiltrated this dense thicket of flags or streamers. The sacking scalp was stained sooty black. The crimsons and scarlets, the green tartans and mustard blotches all had a grain of fine, fine black specks. I sometimes thought of the peg-rug as a bed of ribbon seaweed. The soot was like the silted sand in which it lay.

Not that we did not brush and brush ceaselessly, to cleanse our firesides of this falling, sifting black dust. It rises lightly, and falls where it was, it whirls briefly, when disturbed, and particles may settle on one's own hair and scalp, a soot-plug for every pore in the skin of the hands. You can only collect so much; the rest is displaced, volatile, recurring. This must be the reason why we spent so much time—every morning—making the black front of the black stove blacker with black-lead. To disguise and tame the soot.

"Black-lead" was not lead, but a mixture of plumbago, graphite, and iron filings. It came as a stiff paste, and was spread across, and worked into all the black surfaces, avoiding the brassy ones of course, and then buffed and polished and made even with brushes of different densities, and pads of flannel. It was worked into every crevice of every boss on that ornate casting, and then removed again—the job was very badly done if any sludge of polish could be found encrusted around the leaves and petals of the black floral swags along the doors. I remember the phoenix, who must, I think, have been the trademark of that particular furnace. It sat, staring savagely to the left, on a nest of carved crossed branches, surrounded by an elaborate ascending spiral of fat flames with pointed tongues. It was all blackest black, the feathered bird, the burning pyre, the kindled wood, the bright angry eye, the curved beak.

The black-lead gave a most beautiful, subtle and gentle sheen to the blackness of the stove. It was not like boot-blacking, which produced a mirror-like lacquer. The high content of graphite, the scattering of iron filings, gave a silvery leaden surface—always a *black* surface, but with these shifting hints of soft metallic lightness. I think of it as representing a kind of decorum, a taming and restraining both of the fierce flame inside and the uncompromising cast iron outside. Like all good polishing—almost none of which persists in modern life, for which on the whole we should be grateful—the sheen was built up layer by infinitesimal layer, applied, and almost entirely wiped away again, only the finest skin of mineral adhering and glimmering.

The time is far away when we put so much human blood and muscle into embellishing our houses with careful layers of mineral deposits.

Thinking of black-lead made me think of
its opposite, the white stone and ground
white-stone powder with which we used, daily,
or more often, to emphasise our outer doorsteps
and windowsills. I remember distinctly
smoothing the thick pale stripe along the
doorstep with a block of some stone, but I
cannot remember the name of the stone itself.
It is possible that we simply called it "the
stone." We were only required to stone the step
when we didn't have a maid to do it. I thought
of holystone, blanching stone (perhaps a
fabrication) and a run through the *Oxford
English Dictionary* added whetstone and
sleekstone, a word I hadn't known, which
appears to refer to something used on wet
clothes in the laundry. Finally I found
hearthstone, and hearthstone powder, a mixture
of pipeclay, carbonate of lime, size and
stoneblue. "Hearthstone" was sold in chunks by
pedlars with barrows. I remember the sulphur
in the air from the industrial chimneys of
Sheffield and Manchester, a vile, yellow,
clogging deposit, which smeared windows and
lips alike, and stained the brave white doorsteps
almost as soon as they were stoned. But we went
out, and whitened them again. We lived a gritty,
mineral life, with our noses and fingers in it. I
have read that the black-lead was toxic. I

thought of the white-lead with which Renaissance ladies painted their skins and poisoned their blood. "Let her paint never an inch thick, to this favour shall she come." I remember the dentists, giving us gobbets of quicksilver in little corked test-tubes, to play with. We spread this on our play-table with naked fingers, watching it shiver into a multitude of droplets, rolling it back together again. It was like a substance from an alien world. It adhered to nothing but itself. Yet we spread it everywhere, losing a silvery liquid bead here, under a splinter of wood, or there, in the fibres of our jumpers. Quicksilver too is toxic. No one told us.

Hearthstone is an ancient and ambiguous idea. In the past, the hearth was a synecdoche for the house, home, or even family or clan. (I cannot bring myself to use that humiliated and patronised word "community.") The hearth was the centre, where the warmth, the food and the burning were. Our hearth was in front of the black-leaded range. We had a "sitting-room," but its grate (also regularly black-leaded) was always empty, for no one visited formally enough to sit in its chilly formality. Yet the hearthstone was applied to what was in fact the lintel or *limen,* the threshold. Northerners keep themselves to themselves. The hearthstone stripe on the flagstone step was a limit, a barrier. We were fond of a certain rhetoric. "Never cross my threshold again." "Don't darken my door." The shining silvery dark and the hidden red and gold roar were safely inside. We went out, as my mother used to say, feet first, on our final crossing of that bar. Nowadays, of course, we all go into the oven. Then, it was back to the earth out of which all these powders and pomades had been so lovingly extracted.

Jack Smollett realised that this was the first time his imagination had been stirred by the writing (as opposed to the violence, the misery, the animosity, the shamelessness) of one of his students. He went eagerly to his next class, and sat down next to Cicely Fox, whilst they waited for the others to arrive. She was always punctual, and always sat alone in the pews in the shadow out of the multi-coloured light of the lampshades. She had fine white hair, thinning a little, which she gathered in a soft roll at the back of her neck. She was always elegantly dressed, with long, fluid skirts, and high-necked jumpers inside loose shirt-jackets, in blacks, greys, silvers. She wore, invariably, a brooch on her inner collar, an amethyst in a circle of seed-pearls. She was a thin woman; the flowing garments concealed bony sharpness, not flesh. Her face was long, her skin fine but paper-thin. She had a wide, taut mouth—not much lip—and a straight, elegant nose. Her eyes were the amazing thing. They were so dark, they were almost uniformly black, and seemed to have retreated into the caverns of their sockets, being held to the outer world by the most fragile, spider-web cradle of lid, and muscle, all stained umber, violet, indigo as though bruised by the strain of staying in place. You could see, Jack thought fancifully, her narrow skull under its vanishing integument. You could see where her jaw-bone hung together, under fine vellum. She was beautiful, he thought. She had the knack of keeping very still, with a mild attentive almost-smile on her pale lips. Her sleeves were slightly too long and her thin hands were obscured, most of the time.

He said he thought her writing was marvellous. She turned her face to him with a vague and anxious expression.

"*Real* writing," he said. "May I read it to the class?"

"Please," she said, "do as you wish."

He thought she might have difficulty in hearing. He said:

"I hope you are writing more?"

"You hope . . . ?"

"You are writing *more*." Louder.

"Oh yes. I am doing wash day. It is therapeutic."

"Writing isn't therapy," said Jack Smollett to Cicely Fox. "Not when it's good."

"I expect the motive doesn't matter," said Cicely Fox, in her vague voice. "One has to do one's best."

He felt rebuffed, and didn't know why.

HE READ "How We Used to Black-lead Stoves" aloud to the class. He read contributions aloud, anonymously, himself. He had a fine voice, and often, not always, he did more justice to the writing than its author might have done. He could also, in the right mood, use the reading as a mode of ironic destruction. His practice was not to name the author of the piece. It was usually easy enough to guess.

He enjoyed reading "How We Used to Black-lead Stoves." He read it *con brio,* savouring the phrases that pleased him. For this reason, perhaps, the class fell upon it like a pack of hounds, snarling and ripping at it. They plucked merciless adjectives from the air. "Slow." "Clumsy." "Cold." "Pedantic." "Pompous." "Show-off." "Over-ornate." "Nostalgic."

They criticised the movement, equally gaily. "No drive." "No sense of urgency." "Rambling." "All over the place." "No sense of the speaker." "No real feeling." "No living human interest." "No reason for telling us all this stuff."

Bobby Forster, perhaps the star pupil of the class, was obscurely offended by Cicely Fox's black-lead. His *magnum opus,* which was growing thicker, was a very detailed autobiographical account of his own childhood and youth. He had worked his way through measles, mumps, the circus, his school essays, his passions for schoolgirls, recording every fumbling on every sofa, at home, in the girls' homes, in student lodgings, the point of the breast or the suspender he had struggled to touch. He sneered at rivals, put imperceptive parents and teachers in their place, described his reasons for dropping unattractive girls and acquaintances. He said Cicely Fox substituted things for people. He said detachment wasn't a virtue, it just covered up inadequacy. Come to the point, said Bobby Forster. Why should I care about a daft toxic cleaning method that's thankfully obsolete? Why doesn't the writer give us the feelings of the poor skivvy who had to smear the stuff on?

Tamsin Secret was equally severe. She herself had written a heart-rending description of a mother lovingly preparing a meal for an ingrate who neither turned up to eat it nor telephoned to say she was not coming. "Tender succulent al-dente pasta fragrant with spicy herbs redolent of the South of France with tangy melt-in-the-mouth Parmesan, rich smooth virgin olive oil, delicately perfumed with truffle, mouth-wateringly full of savour . . ." Tamsin Secret said that description for its own sake was simply an *exercise,* every piece of writing needed an *urgent human dimension,* something *vital at stake.* "How We Used to Black-lead Stoves," said Tamsin Secret, was just mindless heritage-journalism. No bite, said Tamsin Secret. No bite, agreed her daughter, Lola. Memory Lane. Yuk.

Cicely Fox sat rigorously upright, and smiled mildly and vaguely at their animation. She looked as though all this was nothing to do with her. Jack Smollett was not clear how much she heard. He himself, unusually, retaliated irritably on her behalf. He said that it was rare to read a piece of writing that worked on more than one level at once. He said that it took skill to make familiar things look strange. He quoted Ezra Pound: "Make it New." He quoted William Carlos Williams: "No ideas but in things." He only ever did this when he was fired up. He was fired up, not only on Cicely Fox's behalf, but more darkly on his own. For the class's rancour, and the banal words in which it expressed that rancour, blew life into his anxiety over his own words, his own work. He called a coffee break, after which he read out Tamsin Secrett's cookery-tragedy. The class liked that, on the whole. Lola said it was very touching. Mother and daughter kept up an elaborate charade that their writings had nothing to do with each other. The whole class colluded. There was *nothing* worse than dried-up overcooked spag, said Lola Secrett.

THE CLASSES TENDED to end with general discussions of the nature of writing. They all took pleasure in describing themselves at work—what it was like to be blocked, what it was like to become unblocked, what it was like to capture a feeling precisely. Jack wanted Cicely Fox to join in. He addressed her directly, raising his voice slightly.

"And why do you write, Miss Fox?"

"Well, I would hardly say I do write as yet. But I write because I like words. I suppose if I liked stone I might carve. I like words. I like reading. I notice particular words. That sets me off."

This answer was, though it should not have been, unusual.

Jack himself found it harder and harder to know where to begin to describe anything. Distaste for the kind of words employed by Tamsin and Lola made him impotent with revulsion and anger. Cliché spread like a stain across the written world, and he didn't know a technique for expunging it. Nor had he the skill to do what Leonardo said we should do with cracks, or Constable with cloud-forms, and make the stains into new, suggested forms.

CICELY FOX DID NOT COME to the pub with the rest of the class. Jack could not offer to drive her home, for the idea of her frail bony form on his motor bike was impossible. He realised he was trying to think of ways to get to talk to her, as though she had been a pretty girl.

The best he could do was to sit next to her in the coffee break in the church. This was hard, because everyone wanted his attention. On the other hand, because of her deafness perhaps, she sat slightly separate from the others, so he could move next to her. But then he had to shout.

"I was wondering what you read, Miss Fox?"

"Oh, the old things. They wouldn't interest you young people. Things I used to like as a girl. Poetry increasingly. I find I don't seem to want to read novels much any more."

"I'd put you down as a reader of Jane Austen."

"Had you?" she said vaguely. "I suppose you would," she added, without revealing whether or not she liked Jane Austen. He felt snubbed. He said:

"*Which* poems, Miss Fox?"

"These days, mostly George Herbert."

"Are you religious?"

"No. He is the only writer who makes me regret that for a moment. He makes one understand grace. Also, he is good on dust."

"Dust?" He dredged his memory and came up with "Who sweeps a room as for thy laws/Makes that and the action fine."

"I like *Church Monuments*. With death sweeping dust with an incessant motion.

"Flesh is but the glass, which holds the dust
That measures all our time; which also shall
Be crumbled into dust.

"And then I like the poem where he speaks of his God stretching 'a crumme of dust from Hell to Heaven.' Or . . .

"O that thou shouldst give dust a tongue to
  cry to thee
And then not heare it crying.

"He knew," said Cicely Fox, "the proper relation
between words and things. Dust is a good word."

He tried to ask her how this fitted into her writing,
but she appeared to have retreated again, after this
small burst of speech, into her deafness.

Wash Day

In those days, washing took all the week. We
boiled on Monday, starched on Tuesday, dried
on Wednesday, ironed on Thursday, and
mended on Friday. Besides all the other things
there were to do. We washed outside, in the
wash-house, which was an outhouse, with its
own stone sink, hand pump, copper with a fire
beneath it, and flagged floor. Other implements
were the monstrous mangle, the great galvanised
tubs, and the ponch. Our wash-house was made
of stone blocks with a slate roof, and houseleeks
growing on the roof. Its chimney smoked, and
its windows steamed over. In winter, the steam
melted the ice. It was full of extremes of watery
climate. As a child, I used to put my face against
the stones and find them hot to touch, or
anyway warmish, on wash day. I pretended it
was the witch's cottage in fairy-tales.

. . .

First there was sorting and boiling. You boiled
whites in the copper, which was a huge rounded
vat with a wooden lid. All the wood in the
wash-house was soap-slippery, both flaked apart
and held together by melted and congealed
soap. You boiled the whites—sheets,
pillowcases, table-cloths, napkins, tea-towels
and so on, and then you used the boiled water,
let down a bit, in the tubs, to wash the more
delicate things, or the coloured things which
might run. You had heavy wooden pincers and
poles to stir the whites in the boiling water;
steam came off in clouds, and a kind of grey
scum formed on the surface. When they were
boiled they went through various rinses in tubs.
There was a hiss and a slopping as the hot cloth
hit the freezing water in the tubs. Then you
ponched it. The ponch was a kind of copper
kettle-like thing on a long pole, full of holes like
a vast tea-infuser, or closed colander. It soughed
and sucked at the cloth in the water, leaving
little bosses of pulled damask or cotton where it
had impressed itself and clung. Then with
pincers—and your bare arms—you hoisted all
the weight of the sheets from one tub to another
tub to another. And then you folded the
streaming stuff and wound it through the
wooden jaw-rollers of the mangle. The mangle
had red wheels to turn the rollers, and a
polished wooden handle to turn the wheel. It

sluiced soapy water back into an under-tub,
or splashed it on the floor. You were also
always pumping more water—yanking the
pump-handle, winding the mangle-handle. You
froze, you were scalded. You stood in clouds of
steam and breathed an air which was always full
of a thick sweat—your own sweat, with the
effort, and the odour of the dirt from the
clothes that was being released into the air
and the water.

Then there were the things you had to pull
the washed clothes through, or soak them in.
There was Reckitt's Blue. I don't know what
that was made of. Because we lived in
Derbyshire I always associated it with blue john,
from the Peaks, which I know is quite wrong,
but is a verbal association which has lingered. It
came in little cylindrical bags, wrapped in white
muslin, and produced an intense cobalt colour
when the little bags were swirled in the blue
rinsing water. What went through the blue
water (which was always cold) were the whites. I
don't know by what optical process this blue
staining made the whites whiter, but I can
clearly remember that it did. It wasn't bleach. It
didn't remove recalcitrant stains of tea, or urine,
or strawberry juice—you had to use real bleach
for that, which smelled evil and deathly. The
Reckitt's Blue went out into the water in little

clouds and fibrils, and tendrils of colour. Like
fine threads of glass in glass marbles. Or blood,
if you put a cut finger in a dish of water. You
couldn't see it very well in the galvanised tubs,
but on days when there wasn't too much we
used to do the blueing in a white enamel
panshon, and then you could see the threading
cloud of bright blue going into the clear water,
and mingling, until the water was blue. Then
you swirled the cloth in the blue water—swirled
it, and squashed it, and punched and *mashed* it,
until it was impregnated with blue, until all the
white glistened in pale blueness. As a very little
girl, I used to think the white cloth and the blue
water were like clouds in the sky, but this was
silly. Because in fact in the sky, the white watery
clouds stain the blue, not the other way round.
It was an inversion, a draining. For when you
held up the sheets, and took them from the blue
water to drain them, you could see the blue run
away and the white whiter, blue-white, a
different white from cream, or ivory, or
scorched-yellow white, a white under blue
dripping liquid that had been changed, but not
dyed.

Then there was starch. Starch was viscous and
gluey, it thickened the washing-water like gruel.
I suppose it was a kind of gruel, if you think of
it. Farinaceous molecules expanding in heat.

Starch was slippery and reminded all of us of substances we didn't like to think of—bodily fluids and products—though in fact, it is an innocent, clean, vegetable thing, unlike soap, which is compressed mutton fat, however perfumed. Cloth slipped into starch, and was coated with it. There were degrees of starching. Very dense, glutinous starch for shirt collars. Light, spun-glass starch for delicate nightdresses and knickers. When you hoisted a garment out of a bath of starch it stiffened and fell into flutes like a carving—or if by mistake you left it lying around, anyhow, and it dried out, it would become solid crumples and lumps, like pleated stones where the earth had folded on itself. Starch had to be ironed damp. The smell of the hot iron on the jelly was like a parody of cooking. Gluten, I suppose. You could smell scorching as you could smell burning cakes. You had a nose for things not as they should be.

Clothes in the process of being cleansed haunted our lives. They were accompanying angels, souls washed white in the blood of the Lamb, surrounding us with their rustle and their pale scent. In the eighteenth century, I imagine, wash days happened once or twice a year, but our time was obsessed with cleansing and had not invented mechanical helpers. We went through an endless cycle of bubble, toil

and trouble, surrounded by an only too visible
inanimate host. They danced in the wind,
fluttering vain arms, raising full-bellied skirts to
reveal vacancy, coiling round each other like
white worms. Indoors, they hung in the kitchen
on long racks, winched up to the ceiling, from
where they then dangled, stiff as boards, like
shrouded hanging men. They lay neatly folded,
before and after ironing, like dead choirboys in
effigy, fluted and frilled. Under the hot iron (on
Thursdays) they writhed and winced and
shrank. My great-aunt's huge shapeless rayon
petticoats flared all colours of the rainbow,
spectral, sizzling russets and air-force blues, shot
with copper, shot with peacock blue. They
melted easily, gophering into scabs which
resolved themselves into pin-holes and were
unredeemable. The irons were filled with hot
coals from the kitchen range. They were heavy;
they had to be watched for soot-smears which
would condemn a garment to an immediate
return to the washpot. Inside them the coals of
fire smouldered, spat and dimmed. The kitchen
was full of the smell of singeing, a tawny smell,
a parody of the good golden cooking smells of
buns and biscuits.

It was hard work, but work was life. Work was
coiled and woven into breathing and sleeping
and eating, as the shirt-sleeves coiled and wove

themselves into a tangle with nightdress ribbons and Sunday sashes. In her old age my mother sat beside a twin-tub washing machine, a mechanical reduction of all those archaic containers and hoists and pulleys, and lifted her underwear and pillowcases from wash to rinse to spin with the same wooden pincers. She was arthritic and bird-boned, like a cross seagull. She was offered a new machine with a porthole, which would wash and dry a little every day, and, it was thought, relieve her. She was appalled and distressed. She said she would feel dirty—she would feel *bad*—if she had no wash day. She needed steam and stirring to convince her that she was alive and virtuous. Towards the end, the increasing number of soiled sheets defeated her, and perhaps even killed her, though I think she died, not from overexertion, but from chagrin when she finally had to admit she could no longer wield her ponch or lift a bucket. She felt unnecessary. She had a new white nightdress which she had washed, starched, ironed, and never worn, ready to shroud her still white flesh in her coffin, its Reckitt's Blue glinting now livelier than the shrunken, bruised yellow-grey of her eyelids and lips.

The creative writing class liked this slightly sinister study of cleanliness no better than its predecessor. They introduced the word "overwritten" into their remorseless criticisms. Jack Smollett reflected, not for the first time, that there was an element of kindergarten regression in all adult classes. Group behaviour took over, gangs formed, victims were selected. There were intense jealousies over the teacher's attention, and intense resentments of any show of partiality from the teacher. Cicely Fox was becoming a "teacher's pet." Nobody had much spoken to her in the coffee breaks before Jack's enthusiasm for her work became apparent, but now there was deliberate cutting, and cold-shouldering.

Jack himself knew what he ought to do, or have done. He should have kept his enthusiasm quiet. Or quieter. He was not quite sure why it mattered to him so much to insist that Cicely Fox's writings were the real thing, the thing itself, to the detriment of good order and goodwill. He felt he was standing up for something, like an ancient Wesleyan bearing witness. The "something" was writing, not Miss Fox herself. She dealt with the criticism of her adjectives, the suggestions for livening things up, by smiling vaguely and benignly, nodding occasionally. But Jack felt that he had been teaching something *muddy*, an illegitimate therapy, and suddenly here was writing. Miss Fox's brief essays made Jack want to write. They made him see the world as something to be written. Lola Secrett's pout was an object of delighted study: the right words *would be found* to distinguish it from all other pouts. He wanted to describe the taste of the nasty coffee, and the slope of the headstones in the graveyard. He loved the whirling nastiness of the class because—perhaps—he could write it.

He tried to behave equitably. He made a point of *not* sitting next to Cicely Fox in the coffee break of the Wash Day session, but went and talked to Bobby Forster and Rosy Wheelwright. His new remorseless writer's conscience knew that there was something wrong with all Bobby Forster's sentences, a limping rhythm, an involuntary echo of other writers, a note like the clunk of a piano key when the string is dead. But he was interested in Bobby Forster, his mixture of jauntiness and fear, his intense interest in every event of his own daily activities, which was, after all, writerly. Bobby Forster said he'd sent away for the entrance forms for a competition for new writers in the literary supplement of a Sunday paper. There was a big prize—£2000—and the promise of publication, with the further promise of interest from publishers.

Bobby Forster said he thought he stood a pretty good chance of getting some attention. "I've been thinking I ought to move on from being a literary Learner Driver, you know." Jack Smollett grinned and agreed.

When he got home, he typed up "How We Used to Black-lead Stoves" and "Wash Day" and sent them to the newspaper. The entries had to be submitted under a pseudonym. He chose Jane Temple for Cicely Fox. Jane for Austen, Temple for Herbert. He waited, and in due course received the letter he had never really expected not to receive—all this was *fated.* Cicely Fox had won the competition. She should get in touch with the newspaper, in order to arrange printing, prize-giving, an interview.

HE WAS NOT SURE how Cicely Fox would react to this. He was by now somewhat obsessed by the idea of her, but did not feel that he knew her, in any way. He dreamed of her, often, sitting in the corner of his caravan with her neat hair, scarfed neck, and fragile, cobweb skin, studying him with her darkly hooded eyes. She was judging him for having abandoned, or not having learned, his craft. He knew that he had called up, created, this unnerving Muse. The real Cicely Fox was an elderly English lady, who wrote to please herself. She might well regard his actions as impermissible. She came to his class, but did not submit herself to his, or its judgement. But she judged. He was sure she judged.

The prize he had so to speak put her in the way of winning was a propitiatory offering. He wanted—desperately—that she should be pleased, be happy, admit him to her confidence.

HE GOT on his motor bike and drove for the first time to Miss Fox's address, which was in a road called

Primrose Lane, in a respectable suburb. The houses there were late Victorian semi-detached, and had a cramped look, partly because they were built of large blocks of pinkish stone, and there was something wrong with the proportions. The windows were heavy sash-windows, in black-painted frames. Cicely Fox's windows were all veiled in heavy lacy curtains, not blue-white, but creamy-white, he noticed. He noticed the pruned rose bushes in the front garden, and the donkey-stoned sill of the front step. The door was also black, and in need of repainting. The bell was set in a brass boss. He rang. No one answered. He rang again. Nothing.

He had worked himself up to this scene, the presentation of the letter, her response, whatever it was. He remembered that she was deaf. The gate to the side-alley round the house was open. He walked in, past some dustbins, and came into a back garden, with a diminutive lawn and some ragged buddleia. And a rotary clothes-drier, with nothing hanging from it. There was a back door, also standing above white-lined stone steps. He knocked. Nothing. He tried the handle, and the door swung inwards. He stood on the threshold and called.

"Miss Fox! Cicely Fox! Miss Fox, are you there? It's Jack Smollett."

THERE WAS STILL NO REPLY. He should have gone home at that point, he thought, over and over, later. But he stood there undecided, and then heard a sound, a sound like a bird trapped in a chimney, or a cushion falling from a sofa. He went in through the back door, and crossed a gaunt kitchen, of which he had afterwards only the haziest recollection—dingy wartime "utility" furniture, a stained sink, hospital-green cupboards, an ancient gas-cooker, one leg propped unsteadily on a broken brick. Beyond the kitchen was a hall, with a linoleum floor, and a curious smell. It was a smell both human and musty, the kind of smell overlaid in hospitals by disinfectant. There was no disinfectant here. The hall was dark. Dark, narrow stairs rose into darkness inside ugly boxed-in banisters. He went on tiptoe, creaking in his biking leathers, and pushed open a door into a dimly lit sitting-room. Opposite him, in a chair, was a moaning bundle with huge face, grey-skinned, blotched, furred with down, above which a few white hairs floated on a bald pink dome. The eyes were yellow, vague and bloodshot and did not seem to see him.

In the opposite corner was an overturned television. Its screen was smeared with something that looked like blood. Next to it he saw a pair of naked feet, at the end of long, stringy, naked legs. The rest of the body was bent round the television. Jack Smollett had to cross the room to see the face, and until he saw it, did not think for a moment that it belonged to Cicely Fox. It was turned into the worn sprigged carpet, under a mass of dishevelled white hair. The whole naked body was covered with scars, scabs, stripes, little round burn marks, fresh wounds. There was a much more substantial wound in the throat. There was fresh blood on the forget-me-nots and primroses in the carpet. It was not nice. Cicely Fox was quite dead.

The old creature in the chair made a series of sounds, a chuckle, a swallowing, a wheeze. Jack Smollett made himself go across and ask her, what has happened, who . . . is there a telephone? The lips flapped loosely, and a kind of twittering was all the answer he got. He remembered his mobile phone, and went out, precipitately, into the back garden, where he phoned the police, and was sick.

The police came, and were diligent. The old woman in the chair turned out to be a Miss Flossie Marsh. She and Cicely Fox had lived together in that house since 1949. Miss Marsh had not been seen for many years, and no one could be found who remembered her having spoken. Nor, despite all the efforts of police and doctors, did she speak, then, or ever. Miss Fox had always been briskly pleasant to her neighbours, but had not encouraged contact, or invited anyone in, ever. No one ever found any explanation for the torture that appeared to have been applied to Cicely Fox, clearly over a considerable period of time. Neither lady had any living relatives. The police found no sign of any intruder, other than Jack Smollett. The newspapers reported the affair briefly and ghoulishly. A verdict of murder was brought in, and the case lapsed.

JACK SMOLLETT'S CLASS were temporarily sub-
dued by Miss Fox's fate. Jack's miserable face made
them uneasy. They fetched him coffee. They were kind
to him.

He couldn't write. Cicely Fox's death had destroyed
his desire to write, as surely as the black-lead and the
wash day had kindled it. He dreamed repeatedly, and
had waking visions, of her poor tormented skin, her
bleeding neck, her agonised jaw. He knew, he had
seen, and he couldn't get down, what had happened.
He wondered if Miss Fox's writing had in fact been a
desperate therapy for an appalling life. There were layers and layers of those old scars. Not only on Miss Fox,
on the mute Flossie Marsh also. He *could not* write
that.

The class, on the other hand, buzzed and hummed
with the anticipated pleasure of writing it up, one
day. They were vindicated. Miss Fox belonged after
all in the normal world of their writings, the world
of domestic violence, torture and shock-horror. They
would write what they knew, what had happened
to Cicely Fox, and it would be most satisfactorily
therapeutic.

The Pink Ribbon

HE HELD THE MASS of hair—long, coarse, iron-grey—over his left hand, and brushed it firmly and vigorously with his right. It was greasy to the touch, despite the effort he and Mrs. Bright had put into washing it. He used an old-fashioned brush, with black bristles in a soft, coral-coloured rubber pad, in a lacquered black frame. He brushed and brushed. Mrs. Bright's black face smiled approval. Mrs. Bright would have liked him to call her Deanna, which was her name, but he could not. It would have showed a lack of respect, and he respected and needed Mrs. Bright. And the name had inappropriate associations, nothing to do with a massively overweight Jamaican home help. He separated the hair deftly into three strips. Mrs. Bright remarked, as she frequently remarked, that it was very *strong* hair, it must have been lovely when Mado was young. "Maddy Mad Mado," said the person in the wing-chair in a kind of growl. She was staring at the television screen, which was dead and grey and sprinkled with dust particles. Her face was dimly reflected in it, a heavy grey face with an angry mouth and dark eye-caverns. James began to plait the hair, pulling it tightly into a long serpent. He said, as he often said, that hairs thickened with age, they got stronger. Hairs in the nostrils, hairs on the heavy chin, grasses on a rock-face.

Mrs. Bright, who knew the answer, asked what colour it had been, and was told that it had been fine, and coal-black. Blacker than yours, said James Ennis to Deanna Bright. Black as night. He combed and twisted. So deft he was, for a man, indeed for anyone, said Mrs. Bright. I was trained to do for myself, said James. In the Air Force, in the War. He came to the tail of the plait, and twisted an elastic band round it, three times. The woman in the chair winced and wriggled. James patted her shoulder. She was wearing a towelling gown, pinned at the neck with a nappy-pin for safety. It was white, which, although it showed every mark, was convenient to boil, in case of accidents, which happened constantly, of every description.

Mrs. Bright watched James with approval, as he came to the end of the hair dressing. The pinning up of the fat coil, the precise insertion of thick steel hair-pins. And finally, the attachment of the crisp pink ribbon. A really pretty pink ribbon. A sweet colour, fresh. A lovely colour, she said, as she always said.

"Yes," said James.

"You are a real kind man," said Deanna Bright. The person in the chair plucked at the ribbon.

"No, love," said Deanna Bright. "Have this." She handed her a silk scarf, which Mado fingered dubiously. "They like to touch soft things. I give a lot of them soft toys. They take comfort in them. Some folk will tell you it's because they're in their second childhood, but that's not it. This is an end not a beginning, best to keep things straight. But it calms them to hold on, to stroke, to touch, isn't it?"

This was the day when Mrs. Bright took over whilst James "slipped out" to go to the library and do a little personal shopping. They took care to "settle" Mado before he left. James turned the television on, to distract her gaze and cover the sound of the door opening and shutting. There was a picture of childish flower-drawings and regulated grassy hummocks. There was smiley music. There were portly coloured creatures, purple, green, yellow, scarlet, titupping and trotting. Look at the little fairies and elves, said James, more or less without expression. "Burr," said mad Mado, and then suddenly clearly, in a human voice, "They try to get her to dance, but she won't." "Look, there's a scooter," James persisted.

Mrs. Bright said,

"Where does she wander, I ask myself."

"Nowhere," said James. "She sits here. Except when she tries to get out. When she rattles the door."

"We are all raised in glory," said Deanna Bright. "When she's raised, she'll be a singing soul. So where is she wandering now?"

"Her poor brain is a mass of thick plaques and tangles of meaningless stuff. Like moth-eaten knitting. There's no one there, Mrs. Bright. Or not much of anyone."

"They took her into a dark a dark darkness and lost her," said Mado.

"Took who, dear?"

"They don't know," said Mado vaguely. "Not much they don't."

"Who's 'they'?"

"Who's they," Mado repeated dully.

"It's no good," said James. "She doesn't know the meaning of words."

"You have to keep trying," said Deanna Bright. "Go out now, Mr. Ennis, now she's watching them. I'll put her lunch together while you're gone."

He went out, carrying his red shopping-bag, and once he was in the street he straightened his back, as he always did, breathing the outside air in great gulps, like a man who has been suffocating or drowning. He walked down streets of identical grey houses to the High Street, waited for his pension in the Post Office, bought sausages, mince and a small chicken in the butcher's and vegetables from the amiable Turk on the corner. These were the people he talked to, the blood-stained butcher, the soft-voiced greengrocer, but never for long, for Mrs. Bright's time was ticking away. They asked after his wife and he said she was as well as could be expected. She was full of life, always one for a joke, said the butcher, recalling someone James barely remembered and could not mourn. A kind lady, said the Turk. Yes, said James, as he always did when he didn't want to argue. He would have liked to go into the bookshop, but there was no time, since he needed to go to Boots, and get his prescriptions, and hers. Things to calm two people whose calm lives were a form of frenzy.

She used to do their shopping. She was the one who went out, as she was the one who had had a network of friends and acquaintances, some of them known to him, many of them not. She had not liked to tell him—no, she had liked not to tell him—where she was going or for how long. He hadn't minded. He was good company for himself. Then one day a stranger had knocked at his door and shepherded his wife into the room, saying that he had found her wandering, that she had seemed to be lost. She was recovered by then, she threw her head back and shrilled with laughter. "Just think, James, I had got so *abstracted,* I'd gone back to Mecklenburgh Square, as if we'd just been out on one of our little outings to survey the damage, after the, after the—" "After the bombing," said James.

"Yes," she said. "But there was no smoke without fire, this time."

"I think she needs a nice cup of tea," said the friendly stranger. It was a moment when James could have *known,* and he had chosen not to. She had always been eccentric.

The queue for prescriptions in Boots was long, and he was sent away for twenty minutes—not long enough for the bookshop, long enough to impinge on Deanna Bright. He wandered around the shop, an old man with a shock of white hair, in a crumpled macintosh. He didn't want to stop near the nursing counter, and found himself aimlessly and unexpectedly in the baby department, amongst different packets of pads and animal-headed toothbrushes. There was a high, shining chrome gibbet hung with the plump, staggering television dolls, purple, green, yellow and red, smiling with black eyes and dark mouths in puppet-mask faces. They were all encased in suffocating polythene. They can't breathe in there, James caught himself thinking, but this was not a sign of madness, no, but a sign of super-sanity, for he had been brooding, as anyone in his position occasionally must brood, he supposed, on what could be done, swiftly, with a plastic bag. They looked benign and inane. He came closer, checking his watch, and read their names, Tinky-Wink, Dipsy, Laa-Laa and Po. They had greyish shiny screens pinned on their round bellies, and antennae on their hooded heads. A symbiosis of a television and a one-year-old infant. Ingenious, after all.

The woman behind the counter—busty, hennaed, bespectacled, smiley—said the Teletubbies were very popular, very popular. "They really *love* them." Could she show him one?

"Why not?" said James.

She took Tinky-Wink and Po out of their shimmery sheaths and pressed their little bellies briskly, which caused them to chirp meaningless little songs. "They each have their own, you know, their signature song, easy to remember, for very little kids. They like remembering things, they like to hear them over and over."

"Do they?" said James vaguely.

"Oh yes. And look how soft they are, and made of sensible towelling, you can get them really clean in a washing machine in no time, if there's any sort of an accident. Durable, they are."

He had a vision of ragged bodies flailing, in a spin cycle. Not the circles of Heaven and Purgatory and Hell, but rag dolls flailing in a spin cycle.

"I'll take one."

"Which one would you like? Is it for a little girl or a little boy? A grandchild? Tinky-Wink is a boy—even though he has a handbag—and so is Dipsy. Laa-Laa and Po are girls. You can't *see* the difference of course. Is it a grandson or a granddaughter?"

"No," said James. He said, "I don't have children. It's for someone else. I'll take the green one. It's a slightly bilious green and the name's appropriate."

Dipsy was detached from his meat-hook and an identical Dipsy slid into view from behind him.

"Shall I gift-wrap him, sir?"

"Yes," said James. That would precisely exhaust the twenty minutes.

They had waited to start the child, until the War was over. And then, after the War, when he had been demobbed, and gone back to teaching classics to schoolboys, the conjured child had refused to enter the circle. It had had names—Camilla, Julius, when they were romantic, Blob and Tiny Tim when they were upset or annoyed. It answered to no name, it refused to be. Hitler took it, she used to say. He shook the parcel, covered with woolly lambs on a blue field. "Dipsy," he said to it. "Dipsy fits the case, we're all dipsy." He wondered if he had been talking aloud in Boots. He looked around. No one was staring. Probably he had not.

He always had to stiffen himself against opening his own front door. He was a self-disciplined man, who had been a good teacher, and a good officer in the Air Force, partly because he was equable. He believed, in a classical way, in good temper and reason. He knew that he himself was a vessel of seething rage, against fate, against age, against, God help him (but there was no God) mad Mado herself, who was not *responsible* for his plight, or for hers, though she felt her own baffled bad temper from time to time, and was ready to blame him. He did not want to go into that captivity, with its sick smell and its lurching violence. As he always did, he took out his keys and let himself in. He even found a grim little smile for Deanna Bright.

Mrs. Bright had given Mado her lunch—spooned soup, fingers of toast, a supermarket custard in a plastic cup. Mado fought being fed, but enough went down, Mrs. Bright said. Before Mrs. Bright, he had left Mado little meals in the fridge. This had ceased when he came home and found her at the table with a meal she had put together. It consisted of a conical heap of ground coffee and a puddle of damp flour, which she was attempting to spoon up with a dry avocado stone. He was still intellectually curious enough at that stage to wonder whether the form of the stone had recalled some primitive memory of the shape of a spoon.

"No, dear," he had said. "That won't do, that's all wrong." And she had struck at him with the pointed end, bruising his cheek, and had swept coffee, flour, and plate, away onto the carpet. This then, was a tale of strangeness he could just about tell to a friend in a pub. It had an aesthetic horror to it that was pleasing. He was past that now, there was nothing left in him that wanted to tell anything to anyone, in a pub or anywhere else.

"How has she been?" he asked Deanna Bright.

"Not difficult. Complaining a bit about too many visitors."

"Ah," said James. He tried a joke. "I wish I knew who they were. I could do with someone to talk to."

"She says they're spies. She says she sent them out

on missions and they pretended to have been killed, but secretly they have got back."

"Spies," said James.

Deanna Bright's face was alive with pity and concern.

"It's surprising how many of them talk about spies, and secret services, and that. I suppose they get distrustful."

"She did send out spies, in the War," said James. "She was in the Intelligence Service. She sent them out to France and Norway and Holland, in boats and parachutes. Most of them didn't come back."

"They hide," said Mado loudly. "They are angry, they mean bad, they mean danger, they want—"

"They want?" said Deanna.

"Lamb cutlets," said mad Mado. "Cold cutlets. Very cold, with sauce."

"She means revenge," said James. "A dish best eaten cold. It's somehow encouraging, when there's any sort of a meaning. They might well want revenge."

Deanna Bright looked doubtful, possibly not knowing the saying, possibly doubting Mado's power to make sophisticated connections. She had once spoken sternly to James when he had referred to the woman in the chair as a zombie. "You don't know what you're saying," she said. "You don't *know* that word. She's a poor creature and a wandering soul. Not one of them."

Now, she crammed her woollen hat onto her

springing hair, and set off to help other fraying souls and bodies.

When James was alone, alone that was with mad Mado, he unwrapped Dipsy and handed it mutely to her. She snatched at the doll, held it up, and stared at its mild little face, turned it over on her knee and fingered the towelling. She said,

"They are waiting for us. We're late. We have to get to the clinic. Or maybe it's the cobbler. Sasha hasn't come *again*. They queued half the day for a bit of pork belly."

Her strong fingers kneaded the doll.

"They wired all the upstairs. They lie there and listen in and make dirty jokes. Sasha thinks it's funny."

At the very beginning he had found the sudden presence of invisible people both grotesque and fascinating. He had been married to a woman—met at university in 1939—who spoke like a radio announcer and never mentioned her family. They had married quickly—he was going into battle, they might either of them be cut off tomorrow—and she had said she had no close family, she was an independent orphan, two of their fellow students as witnesses would do for the wedding party. When her wits wandered now the staircases and cupboards filled up with people, people to be accused and berated, pleaded with and conciliated, people who threatened. To some of these she spoke in a rough Cockney voice, shrill and childish, "don't hit me any more, Ma, I'll be good, I wasn't bad, *don't,* Ma, *don't."* Never much more information. When he asked questions about her mother, she said, "I'm an orphan, I *said."* Then there was Sasha, an undependable friend, of whose existence, past or present, he knew nothing, except that she and Mado were "blood-sisters, you know, we cut our wrists and rubbed it in, rubbed it in, *mingled* the blood, Sasha is the only one and she keeps hiding—" And then there were the wartime ghosts who walked again. Friends bombed in their sleep, friends shot down over Germany, men and women sent out on missions—"Come in Akela, Akela come in—" the old voice beseeched, cracking. He himself was many people. He was Robin Binson, who he had always thought was her lover in 1942, Robin darling, give us a fag, let's try to forget it all. That to him, James, had been what she said lying naked on the counterpane, as the bombs fell. Let's try to forget it all. She had forgotten it all, and it all flew about in threads and fragments.

Before the invisible people, there had been bouts of fear connected with shadowy or inauspicious aspects of the visible. Her own face in a mirror, seen through a doorway, who's *that,* I don't want her here, she means no good. Involuntary cringing before her shadow or his, cast on walls, or shop-windows, in the days when they still went out. And there had been the endless agitated chatter about Intelligence. It was a word, he reflected in his solitude, in the presence of absence, which had always meant a lot to her. At University it had been her highest term of praise. She knows a lot, she works, but she hasn't got the essence of the thing, she's not *intelligent.* Or "I like Des. He's quick. He's *intelligent,*" as though the word was interchangeable with "sexy." Which for her it was, perhaps. They had both been going to be schoolteachers, until the war came. He was a classicist, she had read French and German. When they married she had had to give up the idea of teaching, because married women were not allowed to teach, in the Depression of the 1930s, since they might take work from male breadwinners. Then, as the men volunteered, or were called up, the women had been allowed to take their jobs, even in boys' schools. She had got a good job in a London grammar school. They had both been delighted, at least partly because neither of them enjoyed the gloom into which she was cast by lack of intelligent occupation. He had been jealous, in his camps and billets, and later as he flew around the Mediterranean, of her colleagues in the staffroom. But she hadn't been contented. She'd applied to do real war work, and had vanished into the Ministry of Information, where her colleagues were elegant poets, shadowy foreigners, and expert linguists. Her London was burning and hectic. He had supposed that she would go back into teaching, as he did, once it was all over. But she had developed a taste for Intelligence. She stayed on, always secretive about what she actually *did,* earning more than he did, which he tried not to mind.

THE GREY DAY wore on. He gave her her supper, which she whined about. He took her to the bathroom. Another landmark was when, years ago, he had said, "You just go to the bathroom and I'll get your bed ready." And she had said, staring with her now habitual suspicion,

"Where's that?"

"Where's what?"

"That room you said I'd got to go to. Where is it?"

So he took her by the hand. "Don't *pull.* Wait for Sasha. Sasha's knickers are twisted. *Wait for her.*"

He tried to talk to her still. Very occasionally, she answered. He did not know how much of the time, if any, she knew who he was.

Once or twice, waiting to attend to her washing, leaving her bedroom after tucking her in, he had a vertiginous sense that he himself did not know who he was or where he was, or where he had set out to walk to. Once for a dreadful moment he asked himself where the bathroom was, as the dull rooms went round him like a carousel. At twenty he would have known he was tired and laughed. Now, he asked himself—as he asked himself every time he reassured himself that his keys and his money were safe—was it a beginning?

The Pink Ribbon

WHEN SHE HAD got to bed he sat and tried to read Virgil. He thought that the effort of remembering the grammar and the metrics would in some sense exercise his own brain-cells, keep the connections in there flashing and fluent. O pater, anne aliquas ad caelum hinc ire putandum est animas. He had thought of joining an evening class, even of doing a Masters or a Doctorate, but he couldn't go out, it wasn't possible. Every time he forgot a phrase he had once known by heart, singing in the nerves, he felt a brief chill of panic. Is it beginning? I used to know what the pluperfect of "vago" was. The gruff voice complained from her bedroom and he went to unknot the sheets. He didn't like going to bed himself for he so dreaded being woken.

So he dozed over *Aeneid* VI and heard the ruffle of his own snore. He picked up Dipsy, who had been dropped in front of the television, and with him the pink ribbon, and a few of the steel hairpins. He began abstractedly to drive the hairpins into Dipsy's silver screen in his greenish towelling tummy. He stabbed and stabbed.

IT WAS A QUIET STREET, at dead of night. It had a few midnight windows where the square screenlights flickered. There wasn't much music, or what there was

was respectably contained. People didn't come home late, or natter to each other on doorsteps. So he was surprised to hear running feet in full flight, two pairs, a pursuit. Then his doorbell shrilled. He thought, I don't go down at this time of night, it isn't safe. The bell shrilled more insistently. He heard palms, or fists, beating on the door.

He went down, mostly to prevent Mado being woken. He opened the door, on the chain.

"Let me in. O let me in. There's a huge black man, with a knife, he means to kill me, let me in."

"You could be a burglar," said James.

"I could. But if you don't let me in, I'll be dead. O quick, O *please.*"

James heard the other, heavier feet, and opened the door. She was thin, she slipped in like an eel, she leaned against the door whilst he put back the chain and turned the deadlock. They listened, in the silent stairway. The other feet hesitated, stopped. And then went on, still running, but more slowly.

James heard her panting in the shadow. He said,

"Let me give you a glass of water. Come up."

He lived on the first floor. He led the way. She followed. She sank, gracefully, into his armchair, and buried her face in her hands, before he could see it clearly.

She was wearing black shiny sandals with very high, slender heels. Her toenails were painted scarlet. Her legs were young and long. She wore a kind of flimsy scarlet silk shift, slit up the thigh, with narrow shoulder straps. It was a style the younger James would have identified as "tarty" but he was observant, he knew that everyone now dressed in ways he would have thought of as tarty, but expected to be treated with respect. Her hands, holding her head, were long and slender, like her feet, and the nails were also painted red. Her face was hidden by a mass of fine black hair, which was escaping out of a knot on the crown of her head. He was surprised she could have run so fast, in those shoes. Her shoulders heaved; the silk moved with her panting. He padded into the kitchen and found a glass of water.

She had a sharp, lovely face, with red lips in a wide mouth, and long black lashes under lids painted to look bruised. He asked if he should call the police, and she shook her head, mutely sipping water, sitting more easily in his armchair.

"I didn't think you'd open," she said. "I thought I'd had it. I owe you."

"Anyone would . . ."

"They wouldn't. I owe you."

HE COULD NOT THINK what to say next. It seemed ill-mannered to question her, and she sat, still shivering a little, showing no sign of elaborating her story. He usually had something a little stronger than water, as a nightcap, at this time, he said. Would she care to join him? Whisky, for instance, was good for shock.

He had been a man who attracted women easily, at

least in his RAF days with his gold moustache. He had long ago told himself that he must understand when it was all over and abandon it gracefully. There would have been no problem in offering her a nightcap if she had not been beautiful. He told himself that he would have asked her easily enough if she had been fat and toothy.

"Whisky is what I need," she said lightly. "On the rocks, if you don't think that's vulgar."

"Drink is drink," said James, who indeed never put ice in good whisky.

WHEN HE CAME BACK from the kitchen with the glasses, she was pacing the room, looking at his bookshelves, at the photographs on his desk, at the laundry basket in which Mado's paraphernalia was heaped at night, at the wing chair over the back of which the pink ribbon was carefully laid out for tomorrow, in the seat of which Dipsy sprawled, lime-green and softly smiling. He went across to her and handed her the clinking glass. They raised their glasses to each other. The tendrils of hair in the nape of her briefly bowed neck were still damp. She flicked a scarlet finger across Dipsy and looked a question at James. He turned away, and at the same moment a crash and a howl from Mado's room set him running along the corridor.

Mado stood in her doorway, wound somehow in her sheets, like a toga, or gravecloths. Her teeth were chattering. Her grey hair spilled over her face and shoulders. "You crept into my room," she said, "but you don't respond, you mean to hurt me I know you are a bad man, I live with a bad man, there's no help . . ."

James said, "Hush now, let's get back to bed."

Mado became quite frantic, staring over James's shoulder, making wild signs of warding off violence, cowering and gibbering. Behind James the red silk dress ruffled. He said,

"My wife is ill. I'll need a moment or two."

"Get that out of here," said Mado. "That's a wicked witch, that means *bad* to us all—"

"I'm sorry," said James to his visitor.

"No need," she said, retreating.

IT MIGHT HAVE TAKEN HOURS, or all night, to settle Mado, but that night the life and fight went out of her as the other woman retreated; she allowed herself to be put back into a reconstructed bed, after the necessary visit to the bathroom. James went back, feeling ashamed, for no good reason, and diminished, from civilised host to freak.

"I'm sorry," he said, apologising generally, for life, for Mado, for age, for the fusty smell of his home, for inexorable decline. "I'm sorry."

"Why? You've nothing to be sorry for. You're kind, I can see, it's hard. How long has she been like that?"

The ease of the question drew a sigh of relief.

"Five years since she knew who I was," he said. "I do my best, but it isn't enough. We are neither of us happy, but we have to go on."

"You have friends?"

"Fewer and fewer, as much because I can't stand them as because they can't stand me, that is, her—"

"Have you any more whisky?"

She sat down again and he fetched the bottle. She asked light little questions, and he told her things—things like the avocado stone, things like the Intelligence, and she smiled but did not laugh, acknowledging with her attentive, mobile face the aesthetic comedy, and its smallness compared to the smothering bulk of the whole.

"I'm sorry," he kept saying. "I don't ever talk."

"Don't be," she said. "There's no need. No call to be *sorry.*"

AFTER THE NEXT GLASS she began to roam the room again, the red silk fluttering round her thighs. He thought one compliment would not be misconstrued and told her she was wearing a very fetching dress. This caused her to throw back her head and laugh, freely, lightly, so that then they both froze and listened to hear if Mado had stirred. She went back to the wing chair and picked up the pink ribbon, running it between her long fingers, testing it.

"She doesn't like pink," she told him.

"No," he agreed. "She hates it. She always did. Babyish, she said. Wouldn't wear pink panties or a pink slip. Ivory or ice-blue, she liked. And red."

"She liked red," said the visitor, picking up Dipsy. "You could have got the red one, Po, but you got this bile-coloured one."

"I did it for myself," he said. "A harmless act of violence. It does no hurt."

The young woman swung away from the chair, leaving doll and ribbon in place.

"Dipsy's a daft word," she said.

"Po is even nastier," he said defensively. "Potties it means. Pot-bellies."

"The river Po is the River Eridanus, that goes down to the Underworld. A magical river. You could have got Po."

"What is *your* name?" he asked, as though it followed, a little drunk, mesmerised by the flow of the red silk as she paced.

"Dido. I call myself Dido, anyhow. I'm an orphan. I cast my family off and other names with it. I like Dido. I must go now."

"I'll come down with you, and make sure the coast is clear."

"Thank you," she said. "I'll be seeing you."

He wished she would, but knew she wouldn't.

AFTERWARDS, many things made him doubt that she had really been there at all. Starting with the name she had given herself, Dido, out of his reading. Though equally, she could have picked up his book whilst he was seeing to Mado, and chosen the name of the passionate queen more or less at random. She had known that Po was Eridanus, which he had forgotten, he thought, registering fear at a known fact lost, as he always did. She had some classical knowledge, unexpectedly. And why not, why should a beautiful woman in red silk not know some classical things, names of rivers, and so on? She had known that Mado hated pink, which she could not have known, which Mrs. Bright did not know, which he kept to himself. He must have invented, or at least misremembered, that part of the conversation. Maybe she existed as little—or as much—as Sasha, the imaginary blood-sister. He felt a wild sense of loss, with her departure, as though she had brought life into the room—pursued by death and the dark—and had taken it away again. What he felt for her was not sexual desire. He saw the old man he was from the outside, with what he thought was clarity. His creased face and his arthritic fingers and his cobbled teeth and his no doubt graveyard breath had nothing to do with anything so alive and lovely. What he felt was more primitive, pleasure in quickness. She was the quick, and he was the dead. She would never come again.

In bed that night he was visited—as he increasingly was—by a memory so vivid that for a time it seemed as though it was real and here and now. This happened more and more often as he slipped and lost his footing on the slopes between sleep and waking. It was as though only a membrane separated him from the life of the past, as only a caul had separated him from the open air at the moment of birth. Mostly he was a boy again, wandering amongst the intense horse-smell and daisy-bright fields of his childhood, paddling in trout-streams, hearing his parents discuss him in lowered voices, or riding donkeys on wide wet sands. But tonight he relived his first night with Madeleine.

They were students and virgins; he had half-feared and half-hoped that she might not be, for he wanted to be the first and he wanted it not to be a fiasco, or a worse kind of failure. He hadn't asked her about it until they were undressing together in the hotel room he had taken. She turned to laugh at him through the black hair she was unpinning, catching exactly both his anxieties.

"No there's no one else, and yes, you will have to work it all out from scratch, but since human beings always *have* worked it out, we'll probably manage. We've done pretty well up to now," she said, glancing under her lashes, recalling increasingly complicated and tantalising fumbles in cars, in college rooms, in the river near the roots of willows.

She had always demonstrated a sturdy, even shocking, absence of the normal feminine reticences, or modesty, or even anxiety. She loved her own body, and he worshipped it.

They went at it, she said later, tooth and claw, feather and velvet, blood and honey. This night he relived intimacies he had very slowly forgotten through years of war, and other snatched moments of blissful violence, and then the effacement of habit. He remembered feeling, and then thinking, no one else has ever known what this is *really* like, no one else can ever have got this *right*, or the human race would be different. And when he said so to her, she laughed her sharp laugh, and said he was presumptuous—I *told* you, James, *everyone* does it or almost—and then she broke down and kissed him all over his body, and her eyes were hot with tears as they moved like questing insects across his belly, and her muffled voice said, don't believe me, I believe you, no one else *ever . . .*

And tonight he didn't know—he kept rising towards waking like a trout in a river and submerging again—whether he was a soul in bliss, or somehow caught in the toils of torment. His hands were nervy and agile and they were lumpen and groping. The woman rode him, curved in delight, and lay simultaneously like putty across him.

And his eyes which had watered but never wept, were full of tears.

THE NEXT DAY, he believed he might have called her up from the maze of his unconscious. But Deanna Bright, putting things away in the kitchen, rubbed away traces of scarlet lipstick from a glass he'd thought he'd rinsed, and looked a question.

"Someone was being attacked in the street. I took her in."

"You want to watch out, Mr. Ennis. People aren't always what they seem."

"We need to change her sheets again," he said, changing the subject.

SOMETHING HAD CHANGED, however. He had changed. He was afraid of forgetting things, but now he began to be tormented by remembering things, with vivid precision. People and things from his past slid and hissed into reality, obscuring the stained carpet and the wing-chair in which Mado chattered to Sasha, or turned the lime-green dolly in clumsy fingers. He told himself he was like a drowning man, with his life flashing before his eyes, and stopped to wonder exactly how that would be, would you *see* the quick and the dead before your real staring underwater pupils, or would they wind on a speeded-up film inside the dark theatre of the waterlogged head? What happened to him now, was that as he woke out of a nap over his book, or stumbled into his bedroom undoing his buttons, he saw visions, heard sounds, smelled smells, long gone, but now there to be, so to speak, read and *checked*. Dead Germans in the North African desert, their caps, their water-cans. The old woman he and Madeleine had pushed under the table on the worst night of the Blitz, and revived with whisky when she seemed to be having a heart attack. She had had one red felt slipper with a pom-pom and one bare foot. He saw her gnarled toes, he fitted Madeleine's sheepskin slippers to the trembling feet, he smelled—for hours together—the smell of smouldering London when they went out to survey the damage. Grit in his nose, grit in his lungs, grit of stones and explosives and cinders of flesh and bone. They had walked out after the night of May 10th and seen the damage at Westminster Abbey and the gutted House of Commons, had strolled through the parks, seeing fenced-off unexploded bombs and children sailing boats on the Round Pond. He saw now the fencing and the deck chairs, the rubble and the children.

He remembered the fear, but also the young blood in him driven by the fact of survival and the desire to survive. He had been afraid—he remembered the moan of the sirens, the bang and whine of the big bombs, the grinding drone of the bomber engines, and Madeleine's wild laughter as the crashes were elsewhere. Death was close. Friends you were meeting for dinner, who lived in your head as you set off to meet them, never came, because they were mangled meat under brick and timber. Other friends who stared in your memory as the dead stare whilst they take up the final shape your memory will give them, suddenly turned up on the doorstep in lumpen living flesh, bruised and dirty, carrying bags of salvaged belongings, and begged for a bed, for a cup of tea. Fatigue blurred everyone's vision and sharpened their senses. He remembered seeing a mother and child lying under a bench, arms wrapped round each other, and dreading to stir them, in case they were dead. But they were only homeless walkers, sleeping the sleep of the exhausted.

She did not enter these new windows on lost life, Madeleine. The sound of her laughter, that once, was the nearest thing.

When "this" began, he had known that it required more courage to get up every day, to watch over Mado's wandering mind and shambling body, than anything he, or they, had faced in that past. And he had drawn himself up, like a soldier, to do his duty, deciding that it was in both their interests that he should never think of Madeleine, for his duty was here, now, to Mado, whose need was extreme.

THE FACT THAT HE WAS unsettled unsettled Mado, who became what James and Deanna Bright refrained from calling "naughty" for that implied the impossible second childhood. "Wild" James called it. "Restless" was Deanna Bright's word. She began to break things and to hide things. He found her dropping their silver cutlery, inherited from his parents in a plush-lined black case—piece by piece out of the window, listening to the ring of metal on pavement. The Teletubbies had odd little meals made of pink splats of custard gurgling from a lavender machine, and "toasts" with smiley faces which cascaded from a toaster. Excess food was slurped up by an excitable vacuum cleaner called Noo-noo. The splatted custard (she hated pink) roused Mado to brief bursts of competitive energy and the carpet was covered with milk and honey, with baby cream and salad dressing. And with whisky. She poured his Glenfiddich into the hearthrug. The smell of it recalled Dido but the libation produced no spirit. James bought another bottle. The smell lingered, mixed with the ghostly smoke and ashes of burning London in 1941.

THERE CAME A NIGHT when she reappeared and reappeared after he had settled her, whining in the doorway as he tried to construe *Aeneid* VI. "I can't do it," she said, "I can't get it," but could not say what she could not do or get. For a dreadful moment James raised his hand to slap or punch the moaning creature, and she backed away, bubbling. Time for Teletubbies to go to bed, said James instead, in a jingly voice. He pushed her—gently—into her room, and pushed Dipsy into her arms. She tossed Dipsy back at him, snorting angrily, and turned her face to the wall. He picked up Dipsy by the foot and went back to the

Underworld and its perpetual twilight. He found himself torturing Dipsy, winding his little wrist round, and again, driving hairpins into the terrytowelling plump belly. As long as the little unkind acts were harmless, his rational mind said, stabbing.

The doorbell rang. He waited for Mado to respond—if it disturbed her, he wouldn't open, it would be unbearable. But she was still. The bell sounded again. At the third shrilling, he went down. There she was in the doorway, the dark woman, in the red silk dress, like a poppy.

"I come bearing gifts," she said. "To thank you. May I come in?"

"You may," he said, with clumsy ceremony. "You may have a glass of whisky, if you will."

He imagined the elegant nose wrinkled at the smell of his rooms.

"Here," she said, handing him a box of Black Magic chocolates, tied with a scarlet ribbon. Chocolates out of the cinemas of his youth, which had somehow persisted into the present. "And here," she said, lifting her other hand, "for her. I know she'd rather have the red one. Have Po."

He realised Dipsy and the hairpin were still in his hand. Po was done up in what he thought of as cellophane, a beautiful word, also from those earlier days, related to diaphane, although he knew really that she was smiling out of a plastic bag, also done up with a red ribbon. He put down Dipsy, accepted both presents, put them down on the table, and went to fetch whisky, large whiskies, one on the rocks, one neat.

"I didn't think you'd come back."

"Ah, but I had to. And you live so sadly, I thought you might be pleased to see me."

"O I am. But I didn't expect you."

THEY SAT AND TALKED. She crossed and uncrossed her long legs, and he looked at her ankles with intense pleasure and without desire. He remembered Madeleine, running away on moorland, looking back to make sure he could catch her. Dido asked him polite questions about himself, and turned away those he asked in return, so that he found himself, as the smoky spirit rose in his nostrils, telling her about his life, about the returning folk who occupied his flat, mingling with whoever or whatever mad Mado had conjured up. We are quite a crowd, quite a throng of restless spirits, he said, these days, thick as leaves and only two of us flesh and blood. I find myself in odd times and places, quite out of mind until now.

"Such as?"

"Today I remembered packing a crate of oranges and lemons in Algiers. They were lovely things— golden and yellow and shining—and we chose them carefully, the Arab and me, and packed them in woodshavings and nailed the lid down. And a friend who was a pilot brought them back for her, as a surprise, they couldn't get citrus fruit in the War, you know, they craved for it."

"And when she opened the crate," said Dido, "she could smell the half-forgotten smell of citrus oil and juice. And she pulled away the wood-shavings, and put her hand in, like someone looking for treasure in a Lucky Dip at a village fete. And her fingers came up covered with moss-green powder, a lovely colour in the abstract, the colour of lichens and mould. And she took the mouldy lemon out, in its little nest of silver paper, and looked at the orange below, and that simply dissolved into beautiful pale-green powder, like a puff-ball. And she went on, and on, getting dust every-where, piling them up on newspaper, and there was not one good one."

"That's not true. She said it was a—treasure-chest of delights. She said they were—unbelievably deli-cious. She said she saved and savoured *every one*."

"She was always a great liar. As you always knew. It was a wonderful gift. It had rotted on airfields and in depots. It was an accident that it mouldered. She thanked you for the gift."

"How do you know?"

"Don't you know how I know?"

"I am an old man. I am going mad. You are a phantasm."

"Touch me."

"I daren't."

"I said, touch me."

He stood up unsteadily and crossed the swirling space between them. He put the tips of his fingers on the silky hair, and then he touched, chastely and with terror, the warm young skin of her arm.

"Palpable," he said, finding an arcane word from the humming in his brain.

"You see?"

"No, I don't. I believe I believe you are there." He said, "What else do you know? That I might have known, and don't know."

"Sit down and I'll tell you."

"SHE USED TO SAY, Hitler had destroyed the days of her youth, and the quiet days of her marriage, and the child she might have had. And given her drama—too much drama—and dissatisfaction, and eternal restlessness, so she could never be content. She thought these thoughts with great violence, most especially when she was living the quiet days that were simply a *semblance* of quiet days, a simulacrum of a life, so to speak. Though if a kitchen and a plate of macaroni cheese are a phantasm maybe, just maybe, they are more exciting than when they stretch before you as your settled and invariable fate."

"As it is now," he said. Thinking of custard on the floor.

"The worst time—the most unreal—was his, was

your, embarkation leave. Before you went where you couldn't say where you were going, where the orange groves and the lemons bloomed. So you sat both, day by day, for those two weeks, and she watched the clock ticking, and mended your shirt-collar like a wax doll housewife with her head bent over the darning mushroom in the dusty blue heels. And you went out now and then together to survey the damage—churches burst open like smashed fruit, plate glass glittering on pavements the length of Oxford Street and Knightsbridge, and you talked rather carefully of nothing much, as though there was a competition in banality. And when you left, she knew she was not pregnant, and gave you a little peck on the cheek—*acting* the little English wife—no Romeo and Juliet kissing—and off you went, with your kit-bag, into the dark, temporary or permanent."

"Yes," said James.

"Yes," she said. "And then she lay on the floor and howled like an animal, rolled up and down as though she was in extreme agony. And then she got up and had a bath, and painted her toenails and fingernails with her remaining varnish, and rough-dried her hair, and turned on some soothing music, and became—someone else.

"And then the doorbell rang. And there you were—there *he* was—on the doorstep. She thought it was a ghost. The world was full of the walking dead in those days."

"The embarkation was cancelled," said James, reasonably then, reasonably now.

"So she hit out, at the smiling face, with all her strength."

"And drew blood," said James. "With her wedding ring."

"And kissed the blood," said Dido, "and kissed and kissed the mark her hand had made."

"But we survived," said James. He said, "Coming back, being a revenant, was always dangerous. I remember arriving at night back in 1943 when the V-1s were falling. I remember arriving at night—I'd hitched a lift in a troop-lorry—and being put down near some depot at Waterloo. There weren't any buses or taxis to be had, and the sounds of what might have been them approaching in the blackout were sometimes those damned flying bombs, like monstrous clockwork, that ticked and then went out. And then exploded. And the sky was full of flames and smoke, colours you couldn't see now, because the sky is always red over London and you can't see the stars. Those things didn't need the full moon, like the bombers did, but we still felt uneasy when it was full. It was full moon that night. So I walked, carrying as much of my kit as I could, falling into potholes, and listening for the damned things. And when I'd walked for an hour or two, I saw I was walking in the general direction of a steady blaze. Tongues licking up, that *glow*, brick-dust in the air, walls hot to the touch. And the closer I got to home, the closer to the crater, so to speak. And I came up against barriers, and bucket-chains, and one fire-engine feebly spraying. And I ran. I ran up against the barriers, and the wardens tried to turn me back, and I said, that's my house, my wife's in there. And I pushed someone over, and ran into the dust. And saw the house was a shell. The roof and the bedrooms were rubble on the downstairs rooms. I thought she must be in the shelter, and I started pulling at bricks, and burned beams, and I burned my hands. And they pulled at me from behind, shouting. And I saw the pit in the living-room floor, and there was someone pulling at my collar. So I looked up, and there she was, in a nightdress shredded to ribbons by glass and a fireman's jacket, with her hair burned to a birdsnest and her face black as night with no eyebrows—and sooty hot hands with broken nails—"

"There was nothing left," said Dido. "Except each other." She said, "You said you were Aeneas looking for Creusa in burning Troy. And she said to you, 'I'm not a ghost, I'm flesh and blood.' And they kissed, with soot on their tongues, and the burning city in their lungs. Flesh and blood."

James began to shake. He was exceedingly tired and confused and somehow certain that all this presaged his own death, or madness at least, and if he went mad or died, what would become of mad Mado?

"Who are you?" he said, in a tired old voice. "Why are you here?"

"Don't you know?" she said kindly. "I am the Fetch."

"Fetch?"

She sat in his chair, smiling and waiting, sleek and dark in red silk.

"Madeleine?" said James.

"In a sense. You would never listen to anything about spiritual things. You always made cynical jokes, when it was a question of astrology, or clairvoyance, or the otherworld."

"Astronomy is mystery enough," said James as he always said. "A great mystery. We used to fly under the stars thick as daisies. You can't see them now."

"There are many things in heaven and earth you can't *see,* James. The etheric body can get separated from—from the clay. It can wander in churchyards. It needs to be set free. As she needs to be set free."

"I know what you are telling me," said James. "You must know I've thought about it."

"You don't do it, because you would be set free yourself, and you think that would be wrong. But you don't think of her, or you would know what she wants. What I want."

"Dido," said James, using the name for the first time. "She doesn't know what she wants, she can't rightly want or not want, her skull is full of plaques and tangles—"

"You make me angry," said Dido in Madeleine's voice. "All those young Germans in the war, with their lives in front of them, and their girls and their parents, that was all right, your own young pilots on missions with wonderful brains humming with cleverness and hope and rational fear—*that* was all right. But a miserable hulk decorated with a pink ribbon—"

"You could always twist anything."

"Intelligence. O yes. I could always twist anything."

She stood up to go. James stood up to see her out. He meant not to say anything, to be strong, but he heard his own voice,

"Shall I see you again?"

Black silk hair, red silk dress, anachronistic silk stockings with perfect seams up the perfect legs.

"That depends," said Dido. "As you know. That depends."

The next day, he knew she had been there, for the signs were solid. Lipstick on the whisky glass, beribboned chocolates, little red Po smiling at him in her polythene casing. He imagined that Deanna Bright looked at him oddly. She refused a chocolate when he offered one. She picked up Po with sturdy black fingers.

"Shall I get it out, then?"

"No," he said. "No, leave it in the bag for the present."

"I see you had company again," said Deanna Bright.

"Yes," said James.

Deanna Bright shrugged and left rather early.

On the television, in broad daylight, the Teletubbies were sitting on the end of their casket-shaped cradles, swathed in shimmering coverlets like parachute silk, or those silvery blankets wrapped around those rescued from hypothermia or drowning. They lay down to sleep like nodding ninepins, each snoring his or her differentiated snore. Nightnight Teletubbies said the mid-Atlantic motherly voice in the cathode tubing. Night, said mad Mado, more and more angrily, night, night, night, night, night.

"Come to bed," said James, very gently, adjusting the pink ribbon.

"Night," said Mado.

"Just a rest, for a while," said James.

Acknowledgements

THERE ARE MANY PEOPLE I should like to thank for help with these stories. I am particularly grateful to Danielle Olsen, who made real my imagined work of art with the help of the Wellcome Collection. I am also grateful to Siân Ede, whose knowledge of contemporary art was invaluable, and whose opinions are tough. Dr. Hamish McMichen was most helpful with medical matters—my mistakes are my own. "A Stone Woman" is dedicated to Torfi Tulinius, whose scholarly knowledge of Iceland and love of its landscape made me *see* the country. I am grateful to Dominic Gregory for commissioning "Raw Material" to be read aloud at the Ilkley Literature Festival. Harriet Harvey-Wood, Ignês Sodré, and my editor Jenny Uglow will know what more than one of the stories owes to talking to them. My daughters Antonia and Miranda were helpful with Teletubbies; Miranda also helped with body-piercing.

I am, as always, grateful to my publishers, Chatto and Windus and Vintage, in England, and Knopf and

Acknowledgements

Vintage in the United States. Also to my agents, Peters Fraser and Dunlop in the UK and Sterling Lord Literistic in the States. My assistant, Lindsey Andrews, makes writing possible.

Finally, this book is dedicated to my German translator and to my Italian translators, all good friends and precise readers. Talking to them over the years has changed my writing, and my reading.

Printed in the United States
by Baker & Taylor Publisher Services